Born in Santa Fé, Arge... leading Argentinian wri... 1968, he moved to Pa... literature at the universi... José Saer was awarded Spain's prestigious Nadal Prize for *The Event*.

His work is translated into all major languages and includes *The Witness* and *Nobody Nothing Never*, also published by Serpent's Tail.

Helen Lane, who lives in New Mexico, is one of the most eminent translators from Spanish and French into English. Winner of the National Book Award, Gulbenkian and PEN Club Translation Prizes, she is the translator of Octavio Paz, Luisa Valenzuela, Claude Simon, Mario Vargas-Llosa, and Juan Goytisolo as well as Juan José Saer.

**Also by Juan José Saer
and published by Serpent's Tail**

the investigation

Juan José Saer

Translated by Helen Lane

Library of Congress Catalog Card Number: 98-86408

A catalogue record for this book is available from
the British Library on request

The right of Juan José Saer to be identified as
the author of this work has been asserted
in accordance with the Copyright, Designs
and Patents Act 1988

First published as *La Pesquisa* by
Companía Editora Espasa Calpe, Argentina SA/
Seix Barral, 1994

First published in this edition in 1999 by
Serpent's Tail,
4 Blackstock Mews,
London N4

Website: www.serpentstail.com

Typeset by Avon Dataset Ltd, Bidford on Avon, B50 4JH

Printed in Great Britain by Mackays of Chatham plc

10 9 8 7 6 5 4 3 2 1

To Ricardo Piglia

There, however, in December, night comes on swiftly. Morvan knew this. And because of his temperament and perhaps also because of his *métier*, almost immediately after returning from lunch, from the fourth floor of the Special Bureau on the Boulevard Voltaire, he studied anxiously the first signs of night through the frosty windowpanes and the branches of the plane trees, shiny and bare, belying the promise of the gods, namely that plane trees would never lose their leaves, because it was beneath a plane tree in Crete that the unbearably white bull, with horns in the shape of a half-moon, after having abducted her on a beach in Tyre or Sidon – it doesn't matter which in this instance – raped, as is common knowledge, the terrified nymph.

Morvan knew this. And he also knew that it was when darkness fell that the archaic, worn-out ball of mud, that persisted in turning, displaced the point at which they were moving, he, Morvan, and that place called Paris, taking it farther from the sun, depriving it of its disdainful clarity; he knew that it was at this hour that the shadow that he had been pursuing for nine months, as immediate and yet as impossible to catch as his own shadow, was in the habit of emerging from the dusty attic in which it dozed, preparing to strike. And it had already done so – hang on tight, all of you – twenty-seven times.

People there live more intensely than anywhere else on the planet; they live longer if they are French or German rather than African and, if a man is French, he lives longer, apparently, if he is a.city dweller and not a farmer for example, and if he is from the city – again, according to statistics – he lives much longer if he is a Parisian than if he is from some other city and, if a Parisian, much longer if he is a woman than if he is a man – and there must be some truth to all this, because in Paris there are any number of little old ladies, whether of the aristocracy, the middle class, the lower middle class or the proletariat, shriveled spinsters or free women who have reached old age determined not to lose their proud independence, widows of notaries or of doctors, of tradesmen or of subway trainmen, former fishwives or former professors of drawing or singing, novelists who are still writing, immigrants from Russia or California, elderly Jewish survivors of deportation, and even erstwhile *cocottes* forced to retire by a sterner censor than upright morals, that is to say time: the light of day sees them reappear each morning, dressed to the nines or practically in rags, depending on their class, hesitantly studying the multicolored shelves of the supermarkets, or if the weather is good, sitting on the dark green benches in the public squares and along the avenues, proudly aloof or engaged in lively conversation with some other member of their species, or distributing, in a gesture long since made immortal by postcards, bread crumbs to the pigeons; on a spring morning they can be seen in dressing gowns, their torsos leaning out over empty space at a sixth or seventh floor window diligently watering geraniums in bloom. Inside the buildings they can be seen going upstairs or down, slowly and cautiously, with a bag of groceries or a nervous, childish and slightly ridiculous poodle that they are carrying in their arms, which on occasion they speak of to a neighbor using a psychoanalytic terminology that no psychologist would dare apply to a human being today. When they are too far along in years, the nursing home or death whisks them out of sight, yet without their number diminishing thereby, since new graduating classes of widows, of divorcees and of spinsters, after the unreal and overlong interval of what they call active life, having already buried all their relatives and acquaintances, come, unconsciously or resignedly, to fill the seats left vacant.

Their stubborn will to live on, even more mysterious than the concatenation of circumstances that set the world to functioning, and later on themselves – and us as well – within this world, gradually deposits them in their tiny apartments, filled with their odds and ends, doilies, tablecloths embroidered before the second war and threadbare carpets, family furniture and trunks, bathroom cabinets full of medicines, tableware dating back to the last century, yellowish photographs on the walls and on the marble tops of chests of drawers. Some of them still live with their family, but most of them either have no family left or prefer to live alone; statistics – I should like you to know from the outset that this story is true – have proved, moreover, that, at any age, women in general tolerate loneliness better and are more independent than men. The fact is that there are countless numbers of them, and despite statistics that also show, and of course it is a general rule as well, that the rich live longer than the poor, they come from all social classes, and even though by their dress and by the neighborhoods they live in they reveal their particular origins and material means, all of them have in common the traits befitting their sex and their age: their slow gait, their wrinkled hands full of dark veins, the slightly arthritic dignity of their gestures, the evident sadness of their inconceivable last days, their phlegmatic organs and their hesitant, senile reflexes, not to speak of their multiple operations, Caesareans, tooth extractions and removals of gallstones, mastectomies, curettages and resection of cysts and of tumors, or of their rheumatic deformities, neurological disorders, progressive blindness or total deafness, breasts that shrink or shrivel and buttocks that sag, and finally, of the legendary cleft that, literally, expels not only man but also the world, the pink slit that dries up, half closes and dozes off.

And yet, if night swallows them up, as day dawns, as I was saying, they reappear, and those who have not allowed themselves to be gnawed away by despair, poverty, lost illusions, melancholy, flower in mid-morning with their little hats no longer in fashion, their severely tailored winter coats, their discreet touches of rouge, trotting along with their poodles or going down six or seven flights of stairs to go out to buy cat food, canary seed, or the weekly guide listing all the television programs, or perhaps, and why not, go out to a restaurant that they will leave early in the afternoon to go visit some acquaintance who is in the hospital, or more likely still, to the cemetery to tidy up the grave site of a relative, almost transformed now, from matter that they once were, into symbol, idea, metaphor or principle.

It is true that they are an element typical of that city, a bit of local color, like the Louvre, the Arc de Triomphe, or the geraniums on the windowsills to whose existence, it must be granted, that with their little plastic watering cans or their pitchers of matutinal water, they in any event contribute more than anyone else. As a reward perhaps for the labor of preserving and even of multiplying man and world in the network of their much-desired insides, or by sheer chance, because of a random ordering of tissues, blood and cartilage, it has been given to many of them to persist a little longer than others, on the sidelines of time, like those pools in rivers in which the water seems smooth and slow-running, owing to an invisible force that holds back the horizontal current but exerts an inexorable vertical pull toward the bottom.

Although they appear to be harmless, at times they can be irritating, and perhaps the awareness of their own frailness, which paradoxically leads them to believe themselves to be invulnerable, gives their opinions a certain self-assertiveness, which can turn them into the voice of their era that calls the tune, so that in a certain sense their stern remarks at the door of a bakery, their sociological analyses in tearooms, their commonplaces spoken aloud when they are all by themselves in front of the images on their television set, are more revealing of the undercurrents of the present than the speeches of the so-called politicians, specialists in human sciences and journalists. The daily conversation of an old woman with her canary, as she cleans its cage, is perhaps the only serious debate of modern times, not those that take place in legislative assemblies, in courtrooms or at the Sorbonne: having gained, after having lost everything, the privilege of not having anything to lose, a sincerity without self-regard prevails in their oratorical style, which at times is not even expressed through words, but rather through silences and meaningful gestures, through shakings of the head in no way explicit, and through glances in which ardor and detachment are commingled. The common opinion, good or bad, comes forth from their wrinkled lips, at times provoking, in conversational partners less self-satisfied than they, laughter, amazement, and even indignation. We know very well that the popular expression *as my granny used to say* always prefaces some inanity that we laugh at before the words are out, and that in popular song and story old crones generally vie with the devil for superiority. For, all things considered, and even though it is often used to frighten children, the evil nature of old people has something more or less comic about it for the rest of humankind, like a slip of the tongue or an anachronism.

Acquitted of the crime of having an opinion, other dangers lie in wait for elderly women. In the jungle of the cities, just as in the literal one, desire and panic, chance and necessity determine the development of species, and the blind blows dealt out by the tortuous or rectilinear, swift or slow expansion of things also land on little old ladies: brawls between drug addicts, the nocturnal recklessness of novice cat burglars caught hard at work, all-enveloping arguments between con men, and even adolescents on roller skates on the gray sidewalks of the city bereft of a horizon, leave behind a harvest of little old ladies robbed of their money, bloodied and bathed in tears. As we know, it is not the horseman but the horse who sets the galloping pace of the world. But that was not what was weighing on Morvan's mind as he studied, that afternoon in December, almost immediately after returning from lunch, through the bare branches of the plane trees, the swift fall of darkness.

It was two or three days before Christmas, so that it was in the very middle of winter that Morvan was reflecting. The white sky that nonetheless did not brighten the atmosphere promised, as people say, snow. The streets were crowded. Women loaded down with parcels, bags, pine branches and small children, hurried across the white stripes of the pedestrian zones in the streets all around the Place León Blum, of which Morvan, in the place where he was and however far he leaned forward toward the window, could see only a part, although, from having walked all round it in recent months, when the Crime Squad had decided to set up the Special Bureau, he knew by heart every stretch of it, the meeting, not in the form of a star but rather of an asterisk, of the Rue de la Roquette and the Boulevard Voltaire, plus the Rue Godefroy Cavaignac, the Rue Richard Lenoir, and the Avenues Ledru Rollin and Parmentier, that began at various points around the square. Along the entire perimeter, the supermarkets, the bars and the florist shops, the Burger King on one corner, the little square with the carousel at the intersection of the Avenue Ledru Rollin and the western stretch of the Rue de la Roquette, the shoe stores, the pizza parlors and the pharmacies, the greengrocers' and the rotisseries, wove a sort of gleaming colored crown around the somber municipal building, which the strings of lights hanging from its facade, put up especially for the holidays, did not manage to brighten up. Through the windowpane and from the fourth floor, and above all in that special atmosphere that always precedes a heavy snowfall, the going and coming of the somewhat ghostly crowd busy doing

Christmas errands reached him as a silent commotion. The bustling but cheery distant scene of lighted shops, the somber municipal building, the cars waiting at stoplights or crossing intersections at a crawl, the people loaded down with parcels and all bundled up in woolen clothes, the gray facades of the houses and the slate roofs, the bare branches of the plane trees, belying the promise of the gods, and the white sky portending snow at any moment, the *tableau vivant* moving down below, shorn for a few seconds of its causal explanations, had the sharp and at the same time strange intensity of a vision. The great world all about, at once clear and distant, suddenly gave him the impression of having expelled him to an inconceivable exterior of things. But that sudden impression vanished immediately and, as he kept a close watch on the coming of darkness, Morvan continued to reflect on his principal preoccupation.

He felt bitter and clear-minded, confused and alert, tired and determined. In his exemplary twenty-year career in the police force, Captain Morvan had never had the opportunity to confront a situation such as this: the man he was looking for gave him, especially in the months just past, a constant sensation of proximity and even of familiarity, which at times inexplicably discouraged him and at the same time encouraged him to continue to search for him. This sensation had its objective causes, since the space in which the crimes were being committed was gradually being confined within a smaller and smaller circumference around the Special Bureau of the Crime Squad, and in that limitation there was doubtless a significant element, regarding which it was difficult to decide whether it was a question of a persistent chance factor or of a challenge, a sort of rule that the murderer set for himself, a caprice transformed into an obligation like those that madness or art impose upon themselves. It is true that in the months gone by since the first crimes, the murderer had never struck except in the tenth and eleventh *arrondisse-ments*, and that in recent months he had limited himself to the eleventh, thus explaining the establishment of the Special Bureau of the Squad opposite the municipal building, on the Boulevard Voltaire, with him, Morvan, as chief of operations, but the increasing proximity of the crimes with respect to the bureau gave him at times a fleeting, anxious sense of malaise, and whatever the explanation might be, rule or happenstance, compulsive caprice or bold challenge, it seemed to him to be equally disturbing.

He was perhaps too good a police officer. In any event, he sometimes thought that of himself, and occasionally it was his occupation, and the fact of not having fathered any children – which he in no way regretted – that he regarded as the principal causes of the failure of his marriage. In the last year above all, following his separation from Caroline, decided upon by common accord though stemming from an express wish on Morvan's part, the feeling of having reached the age of forty-some only to find himself in the most complete solitude was always accompanied by a suspicion and at the same time by a decision: that the occupation of police officer was the cause of his affective disturbances, but that he could not possibly give it up. His *métier* was not so much a job or a duty as a passion, with all the contradictory excesses that a passion can entail. Not that the abuse of power or brutality or even the venality common among his colleagues had ever tempted him, no, nothing like that: he was the most upright officer – perhaps a little too much so as he himself was sometimes inclined to think a bit ironically – and the most punctilious as regards the law – perhaps a little too much so, as his colleagues thought at times with just a touch of discouragement and even of ill humor – in the entire Crime Squad; and he might have reached a much higher position in the hierarchy if, imitating certain of his classmates at the Police Academy, he had stolen a few hours from his work to devote them, as people say, to politics. But even those who had outranked him and who frequented the antechambers of the ministries and embassies, the mansions of emirs and African dictators, were not unaware of the fact that if there was a difficult investigation that demanded imagination and perseverance, time and rationality, flexibility and stubbornness, an investigation that, moreover, they themselves would not have been at all interested in undertaking, Captain Morvan was able to carry it through and draw from it, whatever they were, the most far-reaching consequences. As is the case with every authentic investigator, whatever the field upon which he brings the passion for truth to bear, it stood out from the seething mass of his other passions, lulled by the impassible drive to know, that in him had no limit save legality and that for that reason made him indifferent to compassion –which apart from his *métier* was not lacking in him – and at times even to justice.

He had not had a difficult life but, rather, a cheerless one – according to an old version of the facts, antedating his experience and his memory, his mother had died as she was bringing him into the world, and inasmuch as his father was a railroad man, a locomotive engineer, and was frequently absent, he had been reared in the country, in the Finistère, by his father's mother. The moment his work permitted, once or twice a month, invariably laden with candy and presents, his father came to see him and to rest for a few days at the home of his mother which, after the disappearance of his wife, was the only home he had. Every so often, during school vacations, his father took him with him on his runs in the locomotive, and when he brought him back, as he was preparing to take off again, he was in the habit of holding him in his arms for a long time, beneath the gaze of the grandmother who, for reasons that Morvan came to understand many years later, would shake her head, with an expression that was not sad so much as annoyed or furious. At the age of eighteen he went off to study law in Paris, but by the following year he had already entered the Police Academy. His father, an old Communist militant who had fought in the Resistance, but who respected him too much to be angry with him, was puzzled by this news, until he understood that unusual aspect of his temperament, the thirst for clarity, the penchant for truth, stronger than the passion for pleasure, than that for his own self and even, as I was saying a moment ago, than that for pity or justice. And after that realization, that sudden awareness, his father had begun to have the vague feeling that he was the son of his own son, attached to him, beyond love that was certain and forthright, by a somewhat fearful respect, guilt and vulnerability. Morvan had a premonition of this, but not until just the year before had he discovered its causes.

Even though they did not live together, the father and the son had never been apart. A sort of shared sensitivity, compounded of seriousness of temperament, mutual protection and silence kept them together. Owing to their respective jobs, weeks and even months could go by without their seeing each other, but never more than ten days or two weeks without their telephoning each other, or without a postcard scribbled between two absorbing tasks, a kind, laconic message in which, beneath the trite phrases comprising it, there palpitated the obscure turbulence of what they had always left unspoken. The death of the grandmother, Morvan's marriage, his father's retirement, had in no way changed that helpless, tacit complicity, which in the father stemmed from an infantile anxiety and in the son from the certainty of a nameless pain. Until, the year before, the secret had come to light.

By his own choice – Morvan and Caroline had tried to dissuade him – his father lived in a home for the aged. His son and his daughter-in-law visited him often, or invited him for stays with them, which the father accepted with the docility of a child allowing himself to be taken, submissive and indifferent, to parks, restaurants and theaters, until the day when, without warning, he packed his bag, offering no explanation, and returned to the old people's home. On his last visit, the father had noticed signs of conflict between Morvan and his wife and, in an unusual state of agitation, had abruptly cut his stay short, and when, a month later, the definite separation took place, Morvan informed him of it in a brief, hurt letter. His father asked him to come see him. As he drove along the expressway toward the Finistère, Morvan already knew that the approaching meeting would bring to light the silent smoldering that had kept them together, like a common wound, for more than forty years.

A week after the meeting, the father committed suicide. When he received the news, Morvan realized that he had already had a secret presentiment of this dénouement and that at the time he had told himself, also in secret, that if his father went through with it, the gesture would be out of proportion to the feelings that the revelation had provoked in his son: because learning that his mother had not died in giving birth to him but had abandoned father and son for another man the moment she had had the strength to stay on her feet and walk out of the maternity hospital, that secret which out of humiliation, prudence, compassion, the father had kept to himself for years, like a burning coal clutched in his fist, that secret that explained the grandmother's fury when father and son had given each other a lingering embrace before each separation, had had no effect on him, Morvan, produced no emotional reaction, as they say, no surprise even, just as if he had read, in a daily paper from forty years before, a news item concerning not his family and his own person, but a vague group of strangers. And not even the news item in its entirety, but merely the headline glimpsed in a moment of distraction on turning a page: *Wife of Communist Member of the Resistance Abandons Husband and Newborn Son for Member of Gestapo.* If, on learning of it, he did not shake his head, clacking his tongue and giving at the same time a little sardonic laugh, it was because his father was telling him the story amid sobs, and because that lovable, austere old man who was living the last hours of his existence was a real presence that he loved and pitied. And as he consoled him, hearing him stammer that – and she herself had said as much before disappearing forever – she was in love with that man, but even though she did not know whose son it was, nor did it matter to her, she had decided to leave just after his birth so as not to have to have a child on her hands, he had the feeling that in the hidden depths of his own being in which those revelations should have set in motion questions, heartache and shocked indignation, the opposite was produced, indifference, fatigue, detached contempt, similar to what might motivate the behavior of an animal species with no relationship to humankind – he, Morvan, who, however, after working for more than twenty years on the Crime Squad, had interrogated the worst criminals of his time and had always treated them, once he had managed to corner them, without gentleness certainly, but also without hatred, although in his heart of hearts he had been horrified by their crimes and, furthermore, had been one of the few police officers of the Squad who had declared himself to be in favor of the abolition of the death penalty. By their acts, he argued, they frighten us and enrage us, but we are not allowed to apply to them the Lex Talionis, so as not to endorse their methods and also so as not to be, as they are, wild beasts. His father's confession had not aroused in him, as they say, either astonishment or a desire for reparation, or even the instinct to see clearly, to know, minutely and exhaustively, everything down to the last detail, as so often happened to him, in order to work out a coherent pattern and from this pattern extract a meaning. Only one image obsessed him, though naturally it did not come from his memory, but appeared, rather, to have been selected from a depth of experience belonging to other men, perhaps to the entire species, with the exception of himself: a beet-red newborn babe, blind and bloody, emerging from between the parted legs of the woman who for nine months had made it, nourished it, and given it shelter and which, once it had managed to free its head from the lips compressing it, comes bursting out, screaming, with its vindictive little fists clenched, causing, as it appears, its whole soft, wrinkled little body, that vibrating, hypersensitive, half-finished mass, still composed almost exclusively of nerves and cartilage, to tremble, that lands in this world to stain with blood the white sheet of the maternity hospital.

Knowing you as I do, you must be wondering what place I occupy in this story, I who seem to know more about the facts than what they reveal at first glance and speak of them and transmit them with the mobility and ubiquity of someone who possesses a multiple, omnipresent consciousness, but I wish to call your attention to the fact that what we are perceiving at this moment is as fragmentary as what I know about what I am telling, but that if tomorrow we were to recount it to someone who was not there or simply call it to our mind, in an organized and linear form, or not even wait for tomorrow, if we simply were to begin to speak about what we are perceiving, at this moment or at any other, the verbal corollary would also give the impression of being in the process of being organized, as it is conveyed, by a mobile, ubiquitous, multiple and omnipresent consciousness. From the beginning I have had the prudence, not to say the courtesy, to present statistics with the aim of proving to you the truth of my story, but I confess that as I see it this convention is superfluous, since by the very fact of existing every story is true, and if one wishes to extract some meaning from it, it suffices to take into consideration the fact that, in order to attain the form that is best suited to it, there is sometimes a need to produce in it, thanks to its elastic properties, a certain compression, certain displacements, and more than a few retouches of its iconography.

The fact is that Morvan, I was saying, found himself, at the age of forty-something, about a year before the moment when we saw him for the first time, after lunch, keeping a close watch on the darkness of a swiftly falling winter night and the contradictorily white sky that portended an imminent snowfall, without a mother, or father, or wife, or children, that is to say, as every so often he himself thought of it, fleetingly and resignedly, completely alone in the world. One good quality protected him: the inability to pity himself. His power of concentration was a sort of magic circle, always illuminated, that confined to the semidarkness outside the formless, confused masses of emotion, fear, anxiety, hatred, self-pity, that might have been capable of disturbing, in the bright zone, his shadow theater. In his capacity for work, there was no stoic element, no fantasy of redemption, but, rather, the organic ability, which seemed natural, to forget himself in order to concentrate, methodically, on what was outside. Knowing him, his colleagues could have applied to his person Nietszche's sarcastic remark about Emmanuel Kant – *That spider's existence!* – but they respected and even were too fond of him to be capable of uttering it, much less of truly thinking it: reserved and affable, Morvan, though demanding when it came to efficiency on the job, was incapable of any authoritarian gesture, and if he was respected and obeyed, he owed it neither to his hierarchical superiority nor to coercion, but to his subordinates' conviction of his intelligence, his perseverance and his probity. Despite the fact that those who knew him slightly sensed within him an undeniable unhappiness, they never reached the point of pitying him, this sadness being so totally absent from his relations with others, and being aware of their own miseries, and despite their leading an apparently more normal existence, they could sometimes reach the point of feeling themselves to be more imperfect than he, like those marionettes that are even more pathetic when one glimpses the strings that control them. Even though he was usually the first to arrive at the Special Bureau and the last to leave, Morvan did not appear to demand the same of his collaborators, and if he took it for granted that they ought to furnish positive results, he did not insist that they should obtain them through his own methods. His lifestyle was, as they say, singular, but that of others was a matter of indifference to him, and if, for example, his office was always clean and orderly, in all truth maniacally so, the fact that in the offices of the others disorder reigned did not seem to cause him the least distress. He practiced an extreme austerity, but the general vitalism, a simulacrum of philosophy, that brimmed over all about him, did not perturb him in the slightest. By contrast or by omission he was a man of his time, and despite his singularity, a fair specimen of the country that had produced him: methodical by virtue of his formal education, rational and level-headed by virtue of his temperament, tolerant by virtue of his inborn sense of decency, modern by virtue of the mercantile power of the society that had shaped him, and this in spite of his frequent contact, because of his profession, with the most horrible perversions of the species, granting the fact that the bright zone of existence is the principal setting toward which, willy-nilly, the world's chaotically dispersed elements ought to converge.

His body was healthy and vigorous, and more out of personal inclination than professional obligation, he engaged in sports – basketball, fencing, swimming – for several hours a week, which brought him as a reward deep, uninterrupted sleep, comparable to that of a rock formation, although every so often a curious dream, always the same one, visited him, leaving him slightly bewildered and somewhat uneasy the next day. By dint of being repeated almost without variation, over a period of many months, it had become familiar to him, and even though it fell short of being a nightmare, he would have liked, without quite knowing why, not to dream it again. The dream took place in a very gray, silent city, enveloped in a crepuscular, omnipresent, uniform darkness, which, in all truth, did not differ much from the real cities he knew, including the city called Paris in which he lived and worked, and which, precisely because of his job, he knew, as the saying goes, like the palm of his hand, and it might even have seemed to him to be the city that he was in had it not been for many isolated details, only certain of which, as always happens in dreams, were clear to him, while the rest remained submerged in the black and viscid region of presentiments. The first of these details was the silence: even though a little less movement was to be seen in the streets than in the cities he knew, it could not be said that it was deserted, and yet the cars, the buses, the subway, the people, behaving almost as usual, moved and acted, in an almost imperceptibly slower fashion perhaps, in an extraordinary silence. I assure you that nothing special happened in that dream, which as I was telling you a moment ago didn't quite turn into a nightmare, and that Morvan strolled without major problems about the city, which to be more exact was not a city properly speaking, but rather, a series of animated scenes that Morvan seemed to contemplate from a ubiquitous and problematical point of view that was inside of them and outside at the same time. The people were not very different either, yet on the other hand not altogether like those of the waking state. And in that very slight difference – and this was one of the most disturbing aspects of the dream though the one which, of all of them, was particularly difficult to manage to pin down – Morvan seemed to glimpse the signs of a terrible revelation regarding the species that populated the cities of his waking state. He had begun to have this dream even before his separation, and when he tried to tell it to Caroline, he found it impossible to discover any meaning in it, and since he began to dream it more and more frequently, what ended up being more and more enigmatic to him was not the dream in and of itself, but its almost identical repetition, and his impression on waking was not that of having been in a different, unknown city, but in the same city as in all his other dreams. The thought did not occur to him that, because of its persistence in the plot of his dreams, that city stood in some remote spot of his inner topography. Because, perhaps, of the crepuscular light that obscured everything, or for some other unknown reason, the places, the architecture, the monuments were unrecognizable and a little out of proportion, either slightly larger or slightly smaller than what they are in the waking state, and in general, particularly the statues standing in the public squares and on the main street corners, difficult to identify: in the case of one of them, which was substantially larger than those with which Morvan was familiar, and therefore ought to have been easier to interpret, it was nearly impossible to determine what it represented. Man, animal, equestrian figure, centaur, satyr, bison, angel or mammoth, the roughnesses of the stone and perhaps erosion betrayed the archaic origin of the monument and made its meaning indecipherable. The same thing happened with certain buildings among the ones that Morvan was sure were temples, without quite knowing why, inasmuch as no recognizable outward sign, least of all their dimensions, allowed one to arrive at that conclusion: neither churches, nor mosques, nor synagogues, nor Greek or Roman temples nor pyramids, the rectilinear, geometrical edifices, long and low-lying, quite numerous and all identical, formed a rectangular enclosure preceded by a much narrower passageway, rectangular as well and adjacent to one of the smaller sides of the first rectangle. Morvan deduced that the dark opening of the passageway, again rectangular, in which there was not even a door, was the entrance leading to the larger rectangle, that is to say the temple properly speaking, and because of the dimensions of the edifice and of the aperture that served as an entry, taking into account the stature of the inhabitants of the city, it could be surmised that the faithful were obliged to crouch down both in order to enter the temple and to remain inside it without bumping their heads against the ceiling. The gods that peopled it had inspired, out of overweening pride perhaps, or perhaps in order to inculcate humility in their believers, that architectonic mortification. When awake, Morvan took pleasure in imagining, not without a certain deliberately affected sense of pathos that by its lack of deference brought to mind the vanity of an artist, that there were many of these gods, that they crawled about in the semidarkness inside the low-lying temples and that, neither malevolent nor benevolent, they controlled at a distance and in secret the thoughts and the acts of their faithful. To tell the truth, everything that Morvan saw in his dreams, though not particularly horrible, caused him not so much anxiety as a vague and persistent revulsion. The relative amount of anxiety properly speaking stemmed from things that did not ordinarily produce anxiety in and of themselves, such as the excessive silence or his inability to specify in what he saw the sources of his sense of differences from things of his waking life, and I must point out once again that despite a very slight distortion and certain problems of legibility of that world immersed in crepuscular shadow, no element of that dream was particularly unusual. A single detail in that gloomy city seemed absurd, not to say grotesque, to him, and in the course of the dream aroused in him a sarcastic indignation, without its implicit horror ceasing to be vaguely felt as a threat. The images adorning the banknotes, instead of being portraits of distinguished persons, represented mythological monsters: Scylla and Charybdis in the smaller ones, the Gorgon in the middle-sized ones and the Chimera in the largest. The drawings that portrayed them inside ovals consisting of intertwined garlands – as though attempting to render them discreet homage – were printed with a wealth of precise details and Morvan, on slipping the bills into his hand so as to contemplate them, wondered whether such respect toward those fearsome creatures did not indicate that they might be the gods whom the inhabitants of the city came to adore, crouching in the dark, in the deliberately cramped dimensions of the temples. There was an obvious incongruity between the unrelenting attention to detail of the drawings and the somewhat vulgar ornamentation of the oval garlands. In the dream, Morvan told himself that that primitive aesthetic, intended to exalt monsters that perhaps forced the inhabitants of the city to humble themselves, revealed in them a rudimentary and, without his quite knowing why, an extremely threatening mentality. Perhaps his fear came, not from the odd elements that differentiated the dream state from the waking state, but from the similarities between the two, which shed an unexpected light on the differences that appeared to reveal, in an indirect way, unsuspected aspects of the waking state. The fact is that, when he awoke from that one dream, which he often dreamed and which was repeated almost without variations, Morvan spent the entire day in a peculiar state, and a slight distortion, which might have been produced either by distance or by proximity, he didn't quite know which, changed his relationship with things. Only on the following night, when, as solid as his own effigy in stone, he dropped straight off to sleep without dreaming anything, was the slight strangeness of the previous night dissipated, and morning found him once again refreshed and resolute, as impermeable to enthusiasm as to dejection.

For a year now, more or less, that equanimity had been more than necessary to him. You have just heard me tell of his personal misfortunes; professionally, the turbulence was no less fierce. In the preceding nine months, the shadow stubbornly bent on striking emerged regularly from the attic in which he dozed, driven by an absurd repetitive impulse, and with maniacal meticulousness, as evidenced by the fact that the details of his staging were each time identical, he acted out as, as they say, his delirious notions, leaving behind a trail of extermination, excess and blood.

In the dim light of dusk, someone, perhaps one ought to call it something, a man or whatever it might be, blending in with the last human shivers of the day that was ending – only to begin again a few hours later, for no known reason, with the first light of dawn – came out to hunt, if we can call it that, and even though it beggars belief because of the fury and the recherché perfectionism of the crimes he committed, frail and defenseless little old ladies. On the winter afternoon when Morvan was standing near the window of his office in the Special Bureau, back from lunch, looking through the bare branches of the plane trees at the white sky that portended snow, he had already done so – I warned you to prepare yourselves for a shock – twenty-seven times.

The solitary man who committed those crimes splashed about without the slightest doubt in the mire of dementia, but for their practical execution he was capable of calling upon the most varied subtleties of cunning, psychology and logic, while at the same time practicing a meticulous expertise in his handling of material reality, as was proved by the total absence of verifiable clues to his crimes and to his movements. The classic temptation to defy the police, common to many megalomaniacal criminals, appeared to be implicit in his modus operandi, and after the establishment of the Special Bureau on the Boulevard Voltaire, his radius of activity, as they say, had grown shorter and shorter, so that the imaginary circumference of the circle around the bureau within which he committed his crimes was narrowing somewhat, to the point that he had committed the last one, number twenty-seven, the week before, with his now legendary skill and his usual impunity, just a few blocks away from the office. Kindly do not attribute the foregoing clichés – a mixture of insanity and logic, a megalomaniacal penchant for risk, dramaturgical and topographical persistence – to the banality of my story, but to that of the obscure mechanism whereby, squeezed into a suffocating steel jacket, he finds himself constrained, for reasons that probably escape even him, to use again and again the same hackneyed soap-opera formulas in his mad program of annihilation.

As I was saying, the first crimes had been committed in the tenth and eleventh *arrondissements,* but the last eighteen victims had all lived in the eleventh. To facilitate matters, the top authorities of the Crime Squad – and naturally of the Ministry of the Interior as well – had decided to set up the Special Bureau on the Boulevard Voltaire, headed by Morvan, who had at his disposal a data-processing expert, two secretaries, six uniformed officers and three plainclothesmen, Inspectors Combes and Juin and Captain Lautret. Like a police headquarters, the Special Bureau operated twenty-four hours a day, and in the spacious apartment provided by the municipality there were even a couple of rooms that could be used as bedrooms and a kitchen which was set up to serve as the pressroom as well. The police headquarters opposite, which operated in an annex of the municipal hall of the *arrondissement,* provided the remainder of the junior staff of the bureau – agents, researchers, messengers, orderlies, assistants – a number of large vehicles such as ambulances or police vans, and common logistical matériel, to be used especially for urgent operations. Morvan thus directed a group of investigators, which we might call a long-term team, and a rapid-intervention emergency squad, and at the same time he was in permanent contact with a network of jurists, informers, politicians, psychiatrists, social workers, physicians, family associations, neighborhood committees and journalists. His liking for solitude suffered a little amid all the commotion, so that he was in the habit of delegating the most visible part of the work to Captain Lautret, who as a consequence had attained a certain celebrity thanks to his statements to the press and his frequent appearances on television. It would be impossible to imagine, as they say, two more different people – I shall tell you about this later on – and yet Morvan had complete confidence in Lautret, who had been, to tell the truth, his best friend for many years. But I don't want to get ahead of myself. For now, what you need to know is that the procedure invented by the Crime Squad, probably the most modern one on the continent and the one that best suited the circumstances, had not produced, in the months that it had been in operation, any results. The five or six suspects arrested, somewhat blindly if the truth were told, had been freed immediately after being interrogated. Accusations, anonymous for the most part, turned out, on being followed up, to be erroneous or slanderous. Telephone calls claiming responsibility that came in the day after each crime proved to be from persons who were either mentally unbalanced, provocateurs or practical jokers. And the two or three pale young men who had probably read too much Dostoevski and came of their own accord to turn themselves in received as punishment for their imaginary crimes nothing more than a few days' observation at the psychiatric hospital. Needless to say, the press, the radio, the television networks and even the movies – two films on the subject were hurriedly shot, one after the twelfth and another after the twentieth crime – not to speak of literature, not only essays but also, although it may be difficult to believe, fiction, magnified the effect, already spectacular in and of itself, of the events. In his capacity as spokesman of the bureau, Captain Lautret, by temperament more sociable than Morvan, and also more tolerant, in the opinion of almost everyone, in the realm of morals, was already a familiar figure to the country's, and even the continent's, television viewers. His relativism, acquired thanks to the rather dubious methods of the Vice Squad, in which he had begun his career, to which one would be obliged to add a police officer's physique more cinematographic than real – he was a gambler, a womanizer, and disdained neither alcohol nor, occasionally, according to what people say, a pinch of cocaine to overcome fatigue – made him a likable figure to his audience, which absorbed with obvious pleasure his communiqués, ignoring the fact, with the most friendly bias toward his person, that his precise sentences, full of legal, psychiatric and police technicalities and larded, here and there, with human considerations and paternalistic orders to ensure public safety, conveyed in essence the fact that, after months of wasting time, energy and money, not the slightest result had been obtained. Snug and cozy on winter nights, in heated apartments against whose windowpanes snowflakes or deluges of ice-cold rain beat in vain, those who in other eras had been born to be persons and had now been transformed into mere consumers, into units of measurement of transnational credit systems, into fractions of points of television audiences and a numerically defined social target of advertising campaigns, absorbed, between two spoonfuls of foodstuffs thawed in the microwave oven, with unjustified relief and inexhaustible credulity, the prerecorded communiqués that the ghostly image of Captain Lautret gave the illusory impression of whispering into the ear of each of them from the magnetic screens, forever on the verge of disintegration, of their television sets. Like all the celebrities of his era, Lautret knew, moreover, that the immense majority of the inhabitants of that continent, and also, doubtless, of the others, confuses the world with an archipelago of electronic and verbal representations so that as a result no matter what happens, if in fact anything still happens, in what was once called real life, it suffices to know what needs to be said on the artificial plane of representations in order for everyone to be more or less satisfied and left with the sensation of having participated in deliberations that changed the course of events. Despite his relativism, his excessively lively temperament – he had perhaps seen too many detective movies, copying his behavior from overly archetypical models, so that his policeman's mannerisms were too obvious, his pace too resolute when he entered a place, and his slap in the face too prompt at interrogation sessions – despite, too, his rather shady dealings during his tour of duty in the Vice Squad, whose golden unwritten rule stipulates that in order to obtain the maximum efficiency police officers and malefactors must behave more or less in the same fashion, Lautret's arguments lacked neither perspicacity nor exactitude, and although at times he hid the fact with rhetorical subtleties, he was capable of clearly distinguishing good and evil. If from time to time he blatantly ignored the nuances, it was perhaps because, by taking an indirect path, he wanted to lead others to think that his apparent ignorance was deliberately aimed at obtaining through more expeditious methods what Morvan's punctiliousness occasionally took rather a long time to harvest. As police officers, they nonetheless had something in common: the years they had been on the Crime Squad had accustomed them to apply, more or less instinctively, a hierarchical scale to crime, which caused them to disdain, and not even take into account as criminals, the petty average ones, so as to deal exclusively with the big ones, with perhaps an excessive interest that many attributed to professional rigor and a few, possibly more perspicacious, to fascination.

Habituated though they were to great criminals, the one they were looking for now, after so many months, did not appear to have, even for them, experts among experts, either parallels or a name. Thus far in the century, no individual had killed as much, or with as much personal style, or as much perseverance, or as much cruelty. His instrument was the knife, which he wielded, not with the subtle skill of the surgeon, but rather – *horresco referens* – with the swift brutality of the butcher. That he should occupy himself solely with defenseless, solitary old ladies made him even more repulsive, and the gratuity of his slaughter – the possessions of the victims remained, almost without exception, untouched – revealed in and of itself, while the details provided further, indeed unfathomably alarming, evidence of dementia. But as I believe I have already told you, at no time did he appear to be lacking in cleverness and reason, and of his passage through the little apartments stained with delirium and blood, there remained not a single trace that might have served to identify him. The man or whatever he might be disappeared behind his acts, as if the perfection of horror that he had attained had given him the stature of the demiurge who exists only in the universes that he creates. In his dealings with others he was most probably persuasive and surely likable, well-dressed and well-mannered, since otherwise there was no way of explaining the fact that he should still inspire confidence in the little old ladies who continued to allow him to enter their apartments despite the general alert that had been broadcast throughout the city, and in the neighborhood in particular, after the first crimes. From this point of view, the orders of the authorities had produced no result despite the fact that, each time that Lautret or someone else appeared on television – and at the pace at which the crimes followed one upon the other this was almost once a week – eloquent, serious to the point of sternness, and at times of supplication, they repeated them. Because of the ease with which he entered and left the apartments, in plain sight of everyone, so to speak, without, paradoxically, anyone noticing him, people began to suspect the male nurses who gave daily injections, the supermarket delivery boys who brought orders around at the end of the afternoon, two or three hospital physicians who made house calls and even a couple of gigolos who had police records owing to their habit of selling their charms to matrons and spending the proceeds with panders of their own sex and approximately their own age. A door-to-door salesman of encyclopedias who got his customers to sign contracts a little too hastily, muddling with shifty and slippery arguments the rather slow thought processes of the ladies, with the aim of talking them into buying *the most intelligent synthesis of contemporary knowledge in twenty-four volumes* according to *Le Monde*, was detained for several hours in the Special Bureau, and regained his freedom only after taking away with him as a souvenir a couple of hard cuffs and threats from Captain Lautret for the unusual nature of his commercial methods. The last victim of this widespread state of suspicion was a tax collector whose mission, in order to combat fraud, was to arrive unexpectedly at people's residences, at the dinner hour, and check to see if they had a television set and had paid the corresponding user's tax. But interrogation of him produced no result: there was not the shadow of a doubt that the man had an *idée fixe*; it had to do, however, not with old ladies but with tax fraud. In the Special Bureau, hypotheses were constructed, remained in precarious balance for a certain time, and then collapsed.

The old ladies appeared to have received their executioner with the most forthright hospitality. In more than a few cases, a bottle of liqueur and two little empty glasses attested to the calm conversation that had preceded the massacre. The climate of confidence between the hunter and his prey was revealed by the fact that the knife was always one of domestic provenance, and many signs observed in a number of cases seemed to indicate that it was the victims themselves who, with the greatest naiveté, went to the kitchen to get the utensil and present it to the butcher. At times, the murderer did not forbear to use torture, and to muffle the screams, he had only to seal the mouths of the old ladies with a piece of adhesive tape or a gag. He stripped them naked and cut them up with a knife while they were still alive, as proved by the copious quantity of blood that had flowed from the wounds and bruises left by the blows. In certain instances, the victims had invited him to dine; it was probably he who had brought the half-empty bottle of Bordeaux still on the table, and to thank the ladies of the house for the pleasant time he had had after having slit their throats or decapitated them, he tore out their eyes or their ears or their breasts and left them nicely arranged on a little dish on the table. The rapes and sodomizations were not always *post mortem*, and everything seemed to indicate that in certain cases in which traces of sperm had been found in their vaginal and buccal cavities, the victims had willingly given in, before the catastrophe, to the visitor's virile charms. There was something scandalous and shocking about the way in which that man, who surely lived in the neighborhood, was capable of serenely leaving home, perpetrating those crimes – sometimes up to three in a single week, and in one instance even two in a single nightmarish night – and then disappearing without a trace, as they say, melting once again into the boundless shadow from which, every so often, impelled by his bloodthirsty, iterative delirium, he emerged. The hypothesis that there was more than one murderer, or that the butcher acted with an accomplice, was inconceivable for two reasons, the first of a psychological and, in the broadest sense of the word, aesthetic, nature, because the personal touch in the twenty-seven crimes was readily discernible, and the second, which to Morvan was the most important, of an ethical nature, because it was impossible for two accomplices, after perpetrating such crimes, to have been able to go on looking each other in the face and lead a normal existence for the remainder of the day. The sun and death: no one, they say, can look them in the face, but as for the nameless distortion that teems on the reverse side of the clear, roiling in confusion as on the bottomless and darker and darker depths of a dull, moving mirror, everyone prefers to ignore it, allowing themselves to be lulled by the dense, bright appearance of things which, for lack of a more subtle nomenclature, we continue to call real.

You would have to have been there and lived in that neighborhood as I have in order to appreciate the atmosphere that reigned, as the saying goes, in those months: any middle-aged man might be stopped on the street by the police, who were in a constant state of alert, and who despite that fact produced no result. Cunning and dementia combined, in the proximity and almost with the surely involuntary complicity of everyone, and particularly that of the victims themselves, seemed inaccessible to logic, to the techniques of police investigation, to error and to punishment. The dragnet of police officers that Morvan let out in the city at dusk each day was hauled in the following morning, discouragingly empty. Since apart from the sperm or a stray hair or two – analyzed *ad tedium* in the laboratories, but of no use because there was nothing with which to compare them – no material trace remained after his massacres, the man whom Morvan and the entire police force of the city were looking for was less a human person than a synthetic, ideal image, made up exclusively of speculative features, without a single empirical element having entered into the composition of it. Everyone more or less agreed with Morvan's thesis, according to which they were dealing with a man in his prime, between thirty-five and forty-five years old, who must regularly engage in some sport since his physical strength was more than considerable, and who probably led a solitary existence, because otherwise his nocturnal disappearances would have no doubt aroused the suspicions of those close to him inasmuch as, in view of the fact that every one of them coincided with the crimes, twenty-seven of them in all, friends and members of his family could not have helped but establish a relationship. His perfect physical fitness was borne out by certain tests run in the laboratories, in the sense that in several instances the quantity of sperm and the places of ejaculation proved unequivocally that in the space of a few hours he had had several consecutive orgasms, and as for his strength, his feats with the knife betrayed the muscles and the sure thrust of the slaughterer, who not only stabs, but also slits throats, decapitates, cuts, opens, separates, slashes to pieces. Although every act of violence, however minimal, is a sign of incipient madness, that of this man, or whatever it was, was clearly evidenced, not by his predilection for murder, or even by his tendency to repeat it to infinity, but by the details with which, in a manner of speaking, he decorated it. In the case of hatred, the crime itself suffices, so the private ritual that he carried out was beyond hatred, in a world contiguous to that of appearances in which each act, each object and each detail occupied the precise place accorded it within the whole by the logic of delirium, valid only for the one who had elaborated the system, and impossible to translate into any known language. We have already seen how his good appearance and charm, his air of a pleasant and decent person, in a word, could easily be deduced from the fact that his own victims opened their door and showed him in, served him a little glass of liqueur or a dinner, and then went to the kitchen themselves to bring him the knife with which he prepared to slit their throats. Several of them were even beyond the least possible doubt still alive, according to the laboratories, when they had given in to his sexual assaults. That he was from the neighborhood could be confirmed by following his itinerary on a map, since as I said after the first crimes discovered in the tenth *arrondissement*, all the rest had been committed in the eleventh, in a more and more limited space, in the immediate vicinity of the municipal hall and of the Place León Blum, which permitted the supposition that the proximity of his victims allowed him to satisfy the homicidal urge that brought him out of his dark cave and that he fell, with his habitual fury, upon the first thing he found within his reach that corresponded to the mad model that he had conjured up for himself, turning himself, for the little old ladies of the neighborhood, through the workings of chance that presided over the encounter of the impulse and its object, into something similar to the neutral and impartial energy of fate.

Morvan made a photocopy of each new entry that was added to the bureau's files so as to complete the duplicate file which he kept at home and which, when he didn't sleep at the bureau, he was in the habit of studying, sometimes until dawn, and sometimes during his entire day off as well. For months, not a single one of his waking moments had been occupied by anything save the strangely close yet ungraspable shadow that emerged, at nightfall, vertiginous and methodical, to strike. Standing near the window, on that December afternoon, back from the restaurant, he looked, with a certain anxiety, at the gray day that was rapidly drawing to a close, through the frosty windowpanes of his office and the bare, shiny branches of the plane trees, in a darker and darker air, despite the electric lights of the shops turned on since morning and the white sky which promised, as they say, an imminent snowfall and which, paradoxically, seemed to accentuate, just above ground level, the darkness of the air. As he has already done so many times, Morvan said to himself, when night comes he will perhaps unhurriedly emerge from his dense, formless semidarkness, and prowling about the almost deserted streets, in the vicinity of the square, will search out, with an idle and ordinary expression, his new prey, approaching it in such a natural and familiar way that, in these threatening times, the old lady will see in him not a danger, but an unexpected protection, warm and manly, to the point that, in order not to deprive herself of his company too soon, she will invite him into her apartment, settling him in an easy chair and offering him a little glass of liqueur and even a good dinner. At a certain moment he, on one pretext or another, asking permission to use the bathroom for example, will undress completely in order not to become bloodstained, in the bathroom or the bedroom, carefully folding his clothes so as to be able to go back out into the street spotlessly dressed later on, and then, having first come through the kitchen, he will return naked to the living room or the dining room, knife in hand, ready to begin his task. For quite some time he will torture the lifeless body abandoned to the knife or the handsaw. He may separate the trunk from the head, or amputate the members, or the breasts, or the ears, or tear out the eyes and carefully arrange them on a little dish on the table or on a shelf, or, beginning at the abdomen, slice the front part of the body open from the pubis to the ribs, taking the organs out and then beginning to separate them and spread them out, poking at them with the tip of the knife or with his gloved fingers, as though searching, amid the enigmatic, still-warm tissues, for the lost explanation of a secret or the prime cause of some immense phantasmagoria. When he tires of digging about and of fulfilling his senseless dreams in very real matter, he will drop the knife, take a shower and get dressed again, studying with an expert eye every last corner of the apartment so as not to leave a single trace of his passage. Then, pausing for a moment near the front door, turning around or perhaps, fleetingly, over his shoulder, he will take one last glance at the apartment, not even as a precaution now, but with amazement rather, or with indifference perhaps, or perhaps without even seeing the ravages left behind by his passage, as though everything had happened in a universe contiguous to that of appearances, to which neither will, nor chance, nor reason, nor space, nor time, nor the senses have access. Immediately thereafter, clean, his hair neatly combed, properly dressed, after having crossed the threshold calmly and unhurriedly, he will lock the door from the outside without making a sound, and, once again outwardly identical to any one of us, he will place the key in his pocket.

"If it's very cold, it has to hurt here when a person drinks it," Tomatis says, pressing down on his temples with the thumb and middle finger of his right hand, and keeping its remaining fingers positioned as follows: the index finger extended diagonally upward, as though it were readying itself to point to an imminent event that will occur on high, and the slightly curled ring and little fingers in front of his left eye, covering it somewhat and pointing, contradictorily, downward.

Pigeon, who has just fallen silent so as to allow the waiter to deposit the first three draft beers of the night on the table, casts a discreet, yet at the same time perplexed and skeptical, glance in Tomatis's direction: perplexed because that statement regarding the proper temperature of the beer in the middle of the story that he, Pigeon, is telling, would seem to denote, on Tomatis's part, a sort of insensitivity to his tale, and skeptical because the statement properly speaking, which Tomatis has uttered with the distracted certainty that characterizes the enunciation of postulates, appears to him to be a purely subjective assertion. A third element adds to his perplexity: the rather folkloric status of national capital of beer, deteriorated in latter years if the truth were told, in which the city has long taken pride, appears to find in Tomatis an unexpected proponent and Pigeon, somewhat alarmed, wonders whether Tomatis, after so many years' separation, owing to his having stayed in the city almost without having ever ventured forth from it, has not allowed himself to be contaminated by a certain provincial ethnocentrism, and is on the point of being disillusioned when, after taking a long swallow and setting down with paradoxical satisfaction his nearly empty glass on the table, Tomatis remarks with a wicked smile:

"It's always been the worst and the coldest beer in the Western world."

"Don't exaggerate," Pigeon says, relieved and pleased.

The third person at the table, a bit intimidated by Pigeon's Parisian aura, yet obviously delighted to be among those present at this dinner, smiles timidly behind his coal-black beard on which, around his mouth, there have remained, after his first swallow of beer, several flecks of white foam. Tomatis has introduced him to Pigeon two weeks before with the following words: *Marcelo Soldi. Pinocchio to his friends. The son of wealthy parents who, at the age of twenty-seven, is the greatest connoisseur of literature in the entire republic.* Although not unaware of the ironic tone of the introduction, the two men introduced both have their own reasons to feel satisfied. In the first place, the fact of their having met each other through Tomatis already seems to them to be a guarantee that they will get along well with each other and share a number of enjoyable moments of conversation during the remaining weeks of Pigeon's stay in the city. And, secondly, their common interest in the famous anonymous dactylogram discovered among Washington's papers, the 815 typed pages of the historical novel *In the Greek Tents,* constitutes in their view a more than sufficient reason to justify the need to introduce them to each other. Two practical elements are conjoined with the specifically hedonistic and worldly factors: Soldi, whom it would not displease to come spend two or three years in Europe – despite Tomatis's ironic comments – would not in principle refuse, should the opportunity present itself, Pigeon as intermediary in order to attain his objective; and Pigeon, for his part, informed by Tomatis that Soldi, thanks to his father's kindly trust in him, has at his disposal whenever he likes not only a car but a motorboat, has hoped to be able to take advantage of them from time to time, if Soldi should propose it, in order to explore, overland or by water, during the remaining weeks of his stay, certain places which, although somewhat out of the way, or perhaps for that very reason, have become for him, after so many years of absence from his native region, almost legendary.

Although it is already the twenty-sixth of March, the weather is still very hot. As it lingers on, summer also appears to have intensified, because of the weeks and weeks of constantly rising temperatures. It is a humid, somewhat stupefying heat. It is not necessary to tire oneself out to feel one's brain become feverish and, as it were, soggy; from the moment one awakens, in the stifling and sweaty dawn, after a few hours' poor sleep, a diurnal lethargy sets in during one's waking hours, clouding, with its grayish steamy vapor, the mind's moving, diaphanous transparency.

Pigeon, who has chosen the month of March to travel, with the deliberate intention of avoiding the height of summer while not depriving himself thereby of the pleasure of savoring the last days of his stay, tolerates with a touch of panic and a secret, contradictory satisfaction the torrid weeks that follow one upon the other. The superstitious fear of not holding up physically under such heat alternates in him with a sort of telluric pride, of the sort that he feared that he had noted a few minutes before in Tomatis with regard to the beer and just as unavowed and childish. The maximum degrees of temperature and humidity, the fluid turbulence of the blue sky at midday and the scorched grass seem to him to confirm his idle and rather infantile belief, now rather vague after so many years abroad, that he comes from a unique place whose well-defined, unalterable features coincide to the millimeter, despite and even owing to time and distance, with the myths that, little by little and unintentionally, he has invented on the basis of them.

The most banal movements cost him incredible effort. Only in the morning, when he awakens, does the awareness of being back in the city produce in him a fleeting euphoria that impels him to leap out of bed, but moments later, as he is preparing the maté, that weak and wavering frame of mind reappears and settles in for the duration of the day, and only with the first drinks of the night does it become attenuated. Héctor, who is again touring Europe, has left him his studio to set himself up in, the large, comfortable white cube, cool and ascetic, resembling the geometrical monochromes painted by its owner, which Pigeon has always suspected of having served his old friend, who paints them with precise and meticulous probity, as a retaining wall, in all likelihood an illusory one, to keep in check both the chaos that teems within and the one, equally infinite and diffuse, that runs riot without.

At some distance from the center of the city, the studio facilitates long walks, but the cruel light that stimulates, imperceptibly, impressions of perdition and even of delirium, leaves him only early morning, late afternoon and nighttime for strolling about streets which in other days have been so familiar to him, and which, nonetheless, he now rediscovers, despite his intermittent pleasure, with a certain surprise. On deciding on the trip, in Paris, several months before, the practical objectives – the sale of his family's few properties, his only tie with the city apart from two or three friends, after Cat's disappearance and the recent death of his mother – allowed him to conceal his nostalgia and impatience, and during the week prior to the flight only wine helped him to lull his anxiety, but after the unreal hours in the plane, beginning with his first strolls about Buenos Aires, a sort of atony, not to say indifference, overtook him: an absence of foreseen emotions, perhaps too eagerly awaited, which causes him to perceive people, places and things with the detachment of one who is a tourist against his will. It is true that he has not come alone: his elder son, a fifteen-year-old adolescent, is with him, and the constant sensation of newness that he attributes to him impoverishes his own sensations. As though they were complementary, their experiences modify each other mutually, and perhaps because of the contradictory nature of the experience that each of them has with respect to that of the other, on entering into contact, or on mingling, like wine and water, they attenuate each other, reciprocally. Only a few days after settling in, Pigeon has been able to observe a curious permutation, inasmuch as it is his son who seems to have adapted himself to circumstances with greater flexibility, who masters better the possibilities of profiting from their stay in the city, whereas the one who was born in it and has spent the greater part of his life in it, looks upon it with the fragmentary and hesitant gaze of a foreigner. His son does not seem to have enough time to make the most, in the company of Alicia, Tomatis's daughter, who is the same age, of all the activities that come his way, swimming, dances, walks, parties, trips to the country, not counting the many hours of deep sleep from which he appears to emerge rested and resolute, whereas for the father, despite the many reunions and the many new experiences, the weeks are a burning, endless, laborious flux. In the slow eddy of the day, the dimension of time does not seem to exist: the world is like a viscous mass imperceptibly spreading, and the creature trapped in the colorless gelatin not only does not struggle, but appears to accept, as the one possible, gradual option, sinking into it.

In the first days after their reunion, Tomatis has studied him discreetly, but also minutely. Although he had been telephoning him from Paris to settle the details ever since the trip had been decided on, Pigeon called him from Buenos Aires almost the moment he got off the plane, apprising him of his arrival in the city three days later, and it was Tomatis who proffered advice concerning the company and the departure time of the bus that they had best take, so that on a hot afternoon – it was still summer – in the first days of the month, Tomatis, his nervous fingers jingling in his pocket the keys of the studio that Héctor had turned over to him before going off to Europe, was waiting, accompanied by Alicia, for them on platform number twenty-nine of the bus

terminal. When Pigeon appeared in the door of the bus –
they had not seen each other for years – they exchanged a
quick, almost secret smile, more visible in their eyes than on
their lips, in which, just as in total darkness a flash of
lightning allows one to see for a fraction of a second,
imprinting on one's retina for a few seconds more and on
one's memory forever, a landscape buried in blackness, the
two of them saw file past, in a sort of common representation
and with an intimacy that dispensed with words, not only
what each of them knew about himself, but also what he
knew or imagined or sensed about the other, that which,
despite time and distance and what there had been no room
for in letters and telephone calls, might be called wasted days,
weeks or years, lost affections, blind and solitary struggle,
halfheartedness and happiness, excitement and failure, hearty,
luminous laughter and the taste of bitter tears.

In his intermittent, discreet attempt to sound him out,
with a mixture of curiosity and solicitude, Tomatis has not
succeeded in getting very much out of him, and after a few
meetings – they had been seeing each other almost every day
– the immediate interest of the subjects they broach, the
fascination of the news they exchange and the intrinsic
pleasure of conversation, as well as the rapidity with which
they have revived old habits, have caused them to lose interest
in what might have been behind Pigeon's bright, imperturbable gaze, his slow and elaborate phrases, his restrained,
thoughtful laughter, his pauses, whether short or endless,
which reveal nothing in particular about his supposedly
mysterious and fathomless inner self. In a certain sense,
Tomatis has finally decided, this is a form of courtesy, and it
seems to him, or at least he hopes, that Pigeon is thinking

and has always thought something similar with regard to his own behavior, that is to say that of Tomatis, who, in order not to overwhelm his interlocutor with complaints, confidences or excessively laborious arguments, assumes a worldly, witty nonchalance.

Without forethought, and without even consulting each other, they have resolved, almost by instinct, to take things as they come, one by one, in the perhaps illusory order in which they present themselves, to weigh them with dispassionate care, and then allow them to go, as they say, on their way. At this point in their lives, and most unexpectedly, the present gives them the impression of being the best of all possible worlds. Their youth seems to them to have remained in a fabulous, archaic zone, more distant and improbable than the dimension in which, in other times, light and insubstantial, the gods levitated, a limbo over and done with, brilliant, inaccessible not only to experience but to memory as well, and despite that, and even though each minute that they live brings them closer, playfully as it were, to nothingness, in which there will disappear everything lived, thought and remembered, from the idea of a universe to the most inconceivably minute of particles, passing by way of each of the intermediate variations that exist between the two, and especially on this hot night at the end of March, they give the impression of being made of solid stuff, robust and carefree, nonchalant, hale and hearty, concentrated on the immediate as is the surgeon on a delicate operation, the athlete on the leap he is about to take, or the sybarite on a sip of cool wine.

Soldi – Pinocchio to his friends, as Tomatis has said at the time of the introduction – for his part has also been observing them during the last two weeks. For several years now, ever since he first approached Tomatis, he has often heard him speak of the Garay twins, one of whom disappeared some eight years before, without a trace, as they say, and the other of whom has lived in Paris for more than twenty. According to Tomatis, they looked so identical that people confused them all the time and they themselves, without having explicitly agreed to do so, contributed, through extremely subtle maneuvers, purely as a joke or for reasons that were obscure even to them, to compounding the confusion. So that, now that he has personally met one of them, it seems to Soldi that the two of them have entered his imagination by way of his experience, and that there has crept into it, probably forever now, the same confusion. The sole exemplar still living of the inconceivable duplicate being that was able to traverse the light of day in the city for so many years, he serves Soldi as an empirical reference for picturing to himself, when he hears Tomatis speak of them, either of the two of them, and even both of them at once, as one and the same doubled image and not as two autonomous, different beings.

On occasion, when he hears Tomatis and Pigeon speaking, even if everything they say amuses and interests him, later on, when he is by himself, he must subject it to a sort of translation: the judgments they express seem to him to be correct at the time he hears them, but in the hours and days that follow he breaks them down into all their basic elements, subjecting each one of them to rigorous examination. The company of those two ironic and imperturbable quadragenarians, already closer if the truth were told to fifty than to forty, charms him, although, or perhaps for that very reason, the conventions that rule their conversation escape him. Even though the relation that he maintains with them, and in particular with Tomatis, with whom he has been meeting almost every week for two years, more or less, has been established in such a way as to place them on an equal footing, Soldi believes he notes that, when they address him, the two friends' tone of voice changes imperceptibly, and their sentences seem to become slightly clearer and more explanatory than the ones, elliptical and full of implications, that they exchange when they are speaking between themselves. Nonetheless, not for anything in the world would he deprive himself of their company, not for anything in the world with the possible exception of a beautiful woman, preferably somewhat older than he, one of those mature women in full bloom to whom the legends of youth attribute an infinite sexual wisdom, capable of filling carnal encounters with obscure magic and secret, unforgettable sensations.

"Even though his name is Soldi and he has lots of money, he's a true nominalist," Tomatis has said to Pigeon on the day of the introduction. And later on, to crown the compliment: "He's a real capo when it comes to thinking."

He has felt gratified by that slightly mocking praise, and grateful as well, since Tomatis is not unaware of his hopes of being able to live abroad for a year or two, in Europe or in the United States, in order to study literary theory, nor of the expectations that have been aroused in him by the arrival of Pigeon, from whom he might be able to get help in carrying out his plans. In his stubborn determination to bring them to fruition it is evident that no professional ambition, as they say, is involved, but, rather, the belief, which appears to give rise to a certain skepticism in Tomatis and reveal in him,

Soldi, a certain ingenuousness, that if he acquires a dependable and detailed knowledge of creativity, the meaning of the mysterious exaltation produced in him ever since he learned to read by that magical linking of words will be revealed to him. The relative freedom afforded him by his family fortune, instead of leading him to multiply it, or to use it to travel, to be a celebrity, or to become a professional race driver – his father, Aldo Soldi, has, among his many businesses a dealership in a German marque of cars – has allowed him to entrench himself in his strange obsession with words, so intimately intertwined, since his childhood, with the most secret depths of his own being, that it is now impossible for him to rid himself of the conviction, as unyielding as a magic spell, that an instrument capable of deciphering the meaning of those iridescent interweavings will be at the same time the key to his understanding, if only fragmentarily, himself.

Another subject arouses the common interest of Soldi, Pigeon and Tomatis. Following the death of Washington Noriega, some eight years before, at almost the same time as the disappearance of Cat, Pigeon's twin brother, his daughter Julia, who had gone to Córdoba to live, separated from her husband and came to Rincón Norte to live in Washington's house. Though relations with her father had been rather difficult, after Washington's death his daughter, who was over fifty at the time, organized her life, without, naturally, any really clear awareness of the situation, along the very same lines as her father's, imitating him in everything that she had always reproached him for: she separated from her husband and went to live by herself, with a woman who did the cleaning for her, in the house in Rincón Norte, making ends meet with a retirement pension from the government and a few sporadic translations of medical books. She had children who were already adults and even grandchildren whom, as had been the case with Washington and herself, she seldom saw. And while, when he was alive, she had distanced herself from him and never let the opportunity to criticize him go by, after his death, when she moved into his house, a belated devotion to her father, if not, indeed, a veritable worship of him, was awakened in her. She endeavored to catalog and put every one of his papers and books in order, and kept the house exactly as Washington had left it. With Washington's old friends who remained in the city, Tomatis, Marcos Rosemberg, Cuello, and others less close to him, relations, to all appearances normal, were in all truth extraordinarily complicated, inasmuch as Julia, who seemed to suffer from retrospective jealousy which she did not altogether succeed in concealing, made them in her heart of hearts responsible for the bad relations that he had had with his family. Rosemberg, who was more or less the same age as the daughter, took things with his customary patience, and Tomatis, who had been born several years after Washington's divorce, and thus had nothing to do with his family affairs, while not forbearing to utter from time to time some sarcastic remark about the situation, handled her with the skill of a devious diplomat, but Cuello, who had been Washington's most faithful friend and had remained at his side till his death, broke with the daughter shortly after she came to live in Rincón Norte, and when he spoke of her before others always referred to her as *that woman*.

All of them were concerned about Washington's papers. Julia collected the ones that were scattered in books, in notebooks, in drawers and in folders, the pages left lying loose and the dusty packets of them, and tried to put them in order, but since she had studied medicine and had little literary or philosophical culture, which was difficult for her to admit, she made scarcely any progress, and owing to her ambivalent feelings toward Washington's old friends, she was unwilling to stoop so far as to ask them for help. One of them had only to make a suggestion to her, and immediately, on the vaguest of pretexts, she rejected it. That situation had obtained for several years when Soldi, whom Tomatis had never heard of, turned up at his house one day with the aim, as he put it, of *having a chat about literature.* It was evident that he had screwed up his courage to ring the bell only with the greatest of difficulty, because after having made that hurried statement he had fallen silent, trying to smile behind his coal-black beard, and although Tomatis had replied *Anything but that,* he had shown him upstairs to the terrace, where they had sat chatting and drinking maté until nightfall, and then gone downtown to have dinner at a restaurant. By the next day they were the best of friends, and a few weeks later Tomatis had had the idea of sending Soldi as a *double agent,* as he put it, to Rincón Norte, thinking that, since Soldi's personal history did not bear the ignominious stain of his having belonged to the circle of Washington's intimate friends during the time that the daughter, abandoned by her father, was withering away in Córdoba, he might be more easily accepted by her, which in fact turned out to be the case. *The bird's been caught,* Tomatis commented, rubbing his hands together, but Soldi, who was too scrupulous and forthright to get mixed up in the intrigues of the two camps, which, deep down, Tomatis, pretending the opposite, approved of, began to devote serious attention to the papers, and instead of throwing fuel on the fire, as they say, tried, without to tell the truth much success, to reconcile them. *He is too honest for anyone to be able to trust him*, Tomatis would often say, laughing at his own pleasantry. Soldi used to go to Rincón Norte every Friday, spending the entire day putting Washington's papers in order. And after three or four work sessions, in a trunk labeled, in Washington's own hand, UNPUBLISHED WORKS (OTHER) he discovered what he called, and almost immediately everyone adopted the word, not the manuscript but the dactylogram.

Only two facts are certain: that the famous dactylogram is a copy, and that its title, *In the Greek Tents,* is posterior to 1918, for it was in that year that César Vallejo wrote the poem from which that title is taken. Of the seventy years gone by since then, in the first forty, or in the first thirty at most, in the dense jungle of those three decades, Soldi and the others know that it is necessary to seek out the weeks, the months, or, and this is the most likely hypothesis, the years in which the novel was written. And as for the author, no sign as yet allows him to be identified. There is no name above or below the title written on the first page, in capital letters between quotation marks, centered at the top of a space left blank, measuring some eight or nine centimeters, after which, single-spaced, with narrow margins, there begins the text of the novel which drags on and on and only comes to an end, with the same ellipsis dots with which it began, 815 dense pages later. The subject is the Trojan war and the place the plain of Scamander, before the walls of the besieged city, where the Greeks have set up camp, as the title announces in a strictly descriptive and documentary tone. The 815 pages are set, from the first to the last, without exception, in the camp. Not once does the narrator move outside the walls, and if the novel ends as the doors of Troy are opening to allow the wooden horse to enter, the episode is seen from afar, by an old soldier who is not aware of the ruse that his own allies have devised. The Trojans are tiny, ghostly, figures, seen strolling in the distance about the ramparts, towers and walls, whom a silent arrow, launched from time to time with a sure aim, from an imprecise point of the plain, just misses. Like everything else that exists, Troy to the narrator seems to be, at one and the same time, close at hand and far away.

Among Washington's friends, the discovery of the dactylogram produced, needless to say, tremendous agitation, and of the many enigmas contained in the 815 pages, the identity of the author is one of the most impenetrable. The daughter maintains that the author in question is her own father, but the word novelist on Washington's lips always had a scornful overtone. What complicates the situation in the extreme is the fact that Julia keeps the dactylogram in a metal box, and does not allow it to leave Rincón Norte or a copy to be made. Soldi was the first to obtain permission to read it, which thanks to laborious negotiation he managed to secure for Tomatis and Marcos Rosemberg as well. The three of them are enthusiastic about the text, and completely at a loss as to the identity of its author and the approximate date of its composition. The one concrete indication in their possession is the rather large characters of the typewriter used to copy the manuscript, in all likelihood a model antedating the Second World War, in good working order judging from the fact that the 815 pages were all written on the same machine, which was already quite well-worn if one takes into account the fact that from the very first lines of the text several poorly aligned keys strike slightly above the imaginary line on which they are leaving their imprint, and that in certain parts of the text, because of the bicolored ribbon, many letters are black at the top and a faded red, owing to an imperfect impression, at the bottom.

Needless to say, for at least a year now, thanks to Tomatis's epistolary comments, Pigeon has been aware of the existence of the novel. He has occupied many hours in Paris speculating about the possible identity of the author, about the probability that there exist, in the city or in the country, or somewhere else, other dusty copies stored in the bottom of a closet or of a valise, and even a survivor of the period who could offer testimony that would shed light on the mystery. A few days after his arrival in the city, in the course of a conversation with Tomatis, the subject was dealt with in detail and they agreed to go, thanks to the diplomatic intervention of Soldi and thanks also to the means of transportation placed at his disposal by his father, to Rincón Norte, to visit Washington's house, which Pigeon had not seen for so long a time, and incidentally have a look at the dactylogram.

And, in fact, this is precisely what they have done during the past day. Soldi had promised to take them by car, but on the very next day after planning the trip, he called Tomatis to propose, if he and Pigeon agreed, going to Washington's not by car via the coast road, but by motorboat via the river. Hence around ten that morning, as the heat began in all truth to be oppressive, Tomatis, Pigeon, Alicia and the little Frenchman, as his new friends in the city call Pigeon's son, met at the entrance to the Yacht Club, on the other side of the lagoon, joining Soldi and the deck hand of the motorboat who had been waiting for them for some time. Beneath eucalyptus trees planted near the shore, Soldi's father's motor-boat, *Blondie*, has also been waiting for them, so to speak, rocking back and forth at the calm cadence, in the torrid morning with no breeze, of the current, bow facing landward, the canvas protecting it already removed by the deck hand. The boat is white, clean, roomy, with its cabin in the middle and at the stern the deck protected from the sun by an awning with green and white stripes; in the refrigerator set into the narrow corner of the cabin that serves as a kitchen, Pigeon, Soldi and the deck hand have stowed everything necessary for a picnic, fruit, hard-boiled eggs, cheese, ham, water, soft drinks, sardines, cans of beer, and after finding places for themselves on the benches on deck, beneath the striped awning, they have waited, with mild excitement owing to their passage from terra firma to the mobility of the water, for the launch to take off, setting, due to the waves it made and continually kept making as it moved forward, maneuvering slowly, the rows of boats tied up along the shore, ghostly, shapeless and blind beneath the canvas covering them, to shaking.

It is only a little less hot in the middle of the river than on the banks, but the movement of the boat and the shadow of the wide green- and white-striped awning has afforded them the enjoyment of a cool little breeze. The water, because of the sun that has been rising higher and higher, glistens on the river banks and all round the boat which, on entering narrower branches of the river, and on forming the wake that opened out in wider and wider angles and in successive waves, has kept shaking the profusion of plants along the banks, little aquatic ferns, reeds, water hyacinths and bulrushes, forming an unstable, tangled transition, at once liquid and solid, between land and water. As the distance between the city and Rincón Norte is not too great, they have proceeded slowly, detouring round islands and up river branches so as not to arrive before the hour agreed on – two-thirty – with Washington's daughter. They have not been able to see, in the entire sky, as far as the visible horizon, a single cloud, any other presence apart from the arid, gleaming sun, surrounded by fusing splinters and spots, as though incandescent matter had been raining down all during their passage. Every so often birds, a yellow-bellied flycatcher, a cardinal, a coaltit, a kingfisher, flushed from the nearby river banks by the purr of the motor, have accompanied, unintentionally, the movement of the boat, emerging suddenly from the branches of the bushes or the dwarf trees covered with climbing vines and taking off in the same direction as they, like a shot, out of confusion or panic. The vegetation, of a washed-out, dull, whitish green, suffering both from the excess of water and the unusual prolongation of summer, has seemed to them to have faded even more as the light mounted in the sky, to pour down from the zenith and penetrate things evenly and, however opaque and massive they may be, make them wavy and translucent. And when they anchor close in to the river bank to eat, in the illusory shadow of several rachitic willow trees, not even getting out of the boat, the cool little breeze on deck from the movement of the boat, beneath the awning with green and white stripes, has ceased to blow so as to dry the drops that are now leaving tortured traces on their sweaty faces. In the direct light from the zenith, for a fair time, even the tense canvas of the awning became translucent, and just as on a screen, the motionless branches of the willows cast their shadow on the green and white stripes, traversed the cloth and were visible from the deck. Only the two adolescents were not sweating: indifferent to the excursion, to the scenery, to the conversation of the adults, to what is exterior in a word, serious, almost sullen, deeply tanned from the many hours spent on the beach, they emerged now and again from their silence to speak in a low voice just between themselves, isolated on the bench at the stern, from which they arose only at lunch time in order to go get a hard-boiled egg or a soft drink in the cabin.

Nonetheless, before and after lunch – a very light one, obviously, because of the heat – the adolescents took a dip, so that the four adults, each of them immersed in the monotonous, frayed drone that flows on endlessly in the depths of each one and becomes more intense in the general torpor of the siesta, have seen them, through half-closed eyelids, raise whitish plumes of water with their kicks and their arm strokes that echoed and re-echoed in the hot, somnolent air and that, as they stirred up the water, formed rhythmical and rapid concentric waves that made the motorboat sway, gently rocking its drowsing occupants. Except for one of them that the deck hand has mixed with orangeade in a paper cup, the cans of beer have remained untouched in the refrigerator: the heat, the constant noise of the motor which, even after it has stopped, has gone on resounding for a good while in their memory, and the fatigue of the incessant day, have been until dusk sufficient alcohol to mist over, with their minute but continuous tremors, the internal transparency that wavers and grows thinner. Around two, breaking, as they say, the sparkling silence and again setting the birds hidden in the branches on the bank to fluttering, the boat has headed once

again for Rincón Norte and finally tied up, slowly and
without the shadow of a false maneuver, alongside a narrow
jetty of wood blackened by the elements, adequate perhaps
for periods of high water, but too tall for the present depths
of the river branch, so that the deck hand has been obliged to
beach the boat, prow first, dispensing with the use of the
wooden jetty, to enable the passengers to land. For at least a
kilometer, they have followed two parallel tracks in the sand,
separated by an intermediate strip covered with dry grass and
white with dust, and have at last begun to make out, amid
the masses of vegetation, bright green and well cared for, of
the patio, the brick-colored roof tiles of Washington's house.
An old woman of mixed blood, in a flower-print house dress,
with a cardboard fan in her hand, a promotional gift from a
store in the city, with the photograph of a movie star on one
side and the name and address of the store on the other,
opened the ironwork gate for them and led them to the house
along a path of irregular white flagstones, laid between
flowerbeds still in bloom in March thanks to the shade of the
trees bordering the entire perimeter of the grounds or
standing, sturdy, well watered and in no particular disposition, at various places in the patio. Washington's daughter
has been waiting for them in the gallery protected from the
sun by climbing plants whose intricately intertwined vines
form foliage so dense that it lets in, through a small number
of openings, only a few luminous sunbeams that leave
irregular dark patches imprinted on the gleaming colored
tiles. Without Washington the house seemed to Pigeon a
little larger than the image of it retained in his memory, and
perhaps for that reason as well a little more desolate. The
daughter, on the other hand, welcomed him with an affability

and a show of pleasure that impressed Pigeon as being exaggerated, because he was seeing her for the first time, but the conclusion that he was later to draw from those excessive signs of hospitality was that, in the heat of the compulsive conflict with the local group of Washington's friends, perhaps without its having even been a conscious decision, she regarded it as a good tactical measure to adopt as her ally someone who was merely passing through the city. Her obliging congeniality toward him was perhaps intended to underline, by contrast, the responsibility of the others for the local skirmishes. But the entire meeting has taken place in a boring, rather solemn, diplomatic ambience. Furtively studying her from time to time, Pigeon has arrived at the conclusion that Julia appears to have inherited her father's straight, silky, white hair, and perhaps something of his Spartan simplicity, and her mother's love of luxury, good breeding, and somewhat conventional elegance. And on entering the library, so familiar to him in other times, on crossing the threshold once again after so many years, he has thought that he perceived an odor of wax, faint but real, which seemed to him to crystallize the change of rule or of influence over the place, the passage from the virile camaraderie of the solitary old man with the rough and fleeting fatality of things, to the constant battle of female will to preserve them, endeavoring to bring to a halt, or better still, force the retreat of, pollution, deterioration, rust, disintegration.

Washington's daughter has brought the metal box, quite a bit larger than a shoe box, but it has been Soldi — Julia calls him Pinocchio — who has opened it, with the key that the mistress of the house has given him. In a semicircle around

Washington's desk, the visitors have contemplated, not moving and not saying a word, Soldi's rather fumbling attempts to insert the little key and then to turn it in the lock, until his efforts brought him a result that he deemed satisfactory, whereupon, leaving the little key in the lock, he removed the cover of the box and carefully took out a thick blue cardboard folder, which he placed on the desk. Once he had opened the folder, the visitors could see for themselves that the dactylogram, in addition to its successive protections of metal and cardboard, had a third one, a sort of large plastic envelope, semitransparent but so thick that it had a yellowish tinge, with a zipper that Soldi resolutely pulled open, and then with his delicate, precise hands took out the tall packet of typed pages, a bit dog-eared and brown now rather than yellow at the edges, singed, one might say, by the steady flame, with no calculable speed, of time that has no end. Once he has set the packet of pages, with no wrapping now, on the table, Soldi has stepped aside, rather solemn-faced behind his beard, crossing his long tanned hands over his abdomen, calm, not to say pleased. Pigeon has taken that pose to be a personal authorization, the intent of which is to encourage him to examine the original, but before going round the table and bending over the packet of typed pages, at his first glance at the rather voluminous parallelepiped that they form, he has immediately realized that Washington cannot be the author, that Washington never could have written a story, and certainly not a story of those dimensions, so that for a few seconds, before finally leaning over the desk, his principal concern has been to keep that conviction from being reflected in his face.

What has attracted, above all else, his attention is the fact that the novel begins with ellipsis dots, and that the first sentence is not really a complete one but, rather, the conclusion of a sentence all of whose supporting arguments are missing:

. . . proof that it is only the phantom that engenders violence.

Setting to one side the entire packet of pages except for the last one, which bears, in the upper right-hand corner, the number 815, Pigeon has been able to see for himself that the final sentence also breaks off and ends, not with a period, but with three ellipsis dots. Then, for several minutes, beneath the mildly expectant gaze of those present, with the impression that all of them would like to name him as arbitrator of a dispute whose real motives not only he, Pigeon, but also, and in particular, each one of the parties involved know nothing of, he has examined the dactylogram, observing that, after all, despite the height reached by the pile of pages, it is not inordinately long, for the characters of the old typewriter that has been used to copy it – the small number of words crossed out with a capital X proves at a glance that it is a copy – are quite large. It is true that the text has been typed out, who knows when, single-spaced, that there is no division into parts, chapters and sections, and that on first sight paragraph indentations are rare; Pigeon has calculated that there is one every thirty or forty pages. The first conclusion that he has drawn from the visual examination of the dactylogram, or from its typographical disposition rather, is that the novel does not include a single dialogue, but later on, once he has gone a little farther into the text, he has been able to see that, in all truth, there are a great many of them, transcribed, however, in indirect form. The sentences are of varying lengths: at times there are short sentences, at times short sentences and long ones alternate, and at times the sentences run on and on, until they reach a length of one or two pages, invariably producing at that point an indentation of the paragraph that follows. Whoever the author may have been – until this very moment when he is sitting at the table drinking the first beer of the night with Soldi and Tomatis, no name has come to his mind – he does not give the impression of clinging, through the systematic use of the short sentence, either to the superstition of effectiveness, or, through the exclusive utilization of interminable periodic ones, to the baroque of vulgarization. Because of a favorable bias, even though he has not yet read the novel, Pigeon attributes to the unknown author a talent for rhythmical modulation thanks to which each sentence is of precisely the right length, being based on the most complete identification of sound and meaning possible, and not on abstract principles of some supposed aesthetic of narration and a so-called vision of the world, as people put it, prior to the moment of writing.

He wished his attention had been more concentrated as he was studying the dactylogram, handling it carefully, but the somewhat indiscreet interest with which the others were observing him, even though he had not exchanged a single look with them, distracted him. The role of arbitrator that the two camps had decided to accord him was so unsettling to him that it interfered with his exactitude, and worse still, with the forthrightness of his opinions. And, instead of having drawn conclusions regarding the text properly speaking, he had uttered a sentence resembling a sound that falls into a dark well, the contents, the depth and even the purpose of which are unknown.

"It may perhaps be necessary to send it to Europe or the United States so that it can be studied with greater scientific precision than it is possible to obtain in Rincón Norte," he has said, giving rise first to a general murmur and then to Washington's daughter's gentle but categorical reply:

"As long as I am alive, it is not leaving this house."

"One of these days, you'll have to bring yourself to having a copy of it made," Soldi has put in, apparently pleased by the exchange of remarks that had just resounded in Washington's room, quite cool because of the deliberate semidarkness that always protected it from the heat outside; the two sentences summed up the situation in what in his opinion was a clear way, sparing him the need to explain to the opposing parties the contradictory nature of the arguments set forth.

"If the paper, the ink or the type of machine were properly analyzed, as well as the text, perhaps more detailed information might be obtained," Pigeon has said, again taking the necessary precautions in order not to give too clear an impression of placing the identity of the author in doubt.

"All that can be done right here," Julia has said.

"I don't believe so," Soldi has said hurriedly, finding it preferable that that contradiction, which because of its transparent good sense any one of those present might have voiced, should be put forward by him, inasmuch as Julia would thereby tolerate it more easily than if it had come from Pigeon or from Tomatis.

"And, to be frank," Julia has said as if she hadn't heard, "I scarcely see the necessity."

"Please excuse me, I'm going to go out to the patio for a moment to get a breath of air," Tomatis has said with the most friendly and carefree intonation that he has been able to extract from his throat choked with indignation.

"Why don't we all do likewise? It must be nice out of doors at this time of day," Pigeon has proposed with the most exquisite urbanity.

Soldi has gathered together the pages of the dactylogram, which he has then very carefully placed inside the plastic envelope, closing the zipper, and, after having put the envelope in the blue folder, placing it in the bottom of the metal box, whose cover he has immediately closed, double-locking it with the little key.

They have all gone out into the patio. In twenty years, it seemed to Pigeon, the trees, some of which were planted in his presence and which on a number of occasions he himself has pruned and watered and, when they were grown, enjoyed their shade as well, not only have grown taller still, but have also given that patio an unfamiliar look. The mulberries, the gum trees, the maples, the ash trees, the acacias or paradise trees, the white or yellow oleanders, the palms and the jasmines, the hedges of privet, passion-flower or honeysuckle, not to mention the fruit trees, fig, lemon, apple, loquat, peach, pear, set out in a special area of the patio, by simply growing, have changed the space in which they are planted, making it different from the image that Pigeon has retained in his memory. That place which he thought he knew by heart seemed to him very different and for that very reason strange, new, slightly disquieting perhaps, as though evidences of a time that continues to flow without us had accumulated in the huge rough trunks and in the disproportionately spreading tops of the trees. Through the openings in the foliage there filtered in patches of light that left their imprint on the well-trod paths, but a dense shadow that retained the coolness and dampness safeguarded the grounds from the stubbornly scorching sun of the last days of March. At a certain moment, Washington's daughter and the three literary specialists, as deep down inside she disdainfully, and with impassive irony, called Pigeon, Soldi and Tomatis, were left by themselves beneath the trees, because the adolescents had disappeared, and in a distant corner of the patio, leaning with interest over certain flowerbeds, the deck hand and the old woman of mixed blood who had received them were talking together. Tomatis had studied with profound interest the branches of a mulberry tree.

"You haven't left us a single mulberry, Julia," he finally said.

"Do you think we were going to wait for you?" Washington's daughter answered him with jovial curtness.

"On the pretext that he's come to catalog the papers, Pinocchio devours every last one of them every time he shows up," Tomatis said.

"I do what I can," Soldi answered, bowing with feigned modesty.

"Rather than the novel, it's the mulberries that you should keep under lock and key, Julia," Tomatis has said.

Pigeon has laughed, not at the aggressive and rather mechanical joviality of the dialogue, but at the tension he perceives behind the words, since he is not unaware of the conflict that for some time has set the two speakers at odds.

"Would you like me to have some maté made for you?"

Julia asked, leading Pigeon to think that in her way of phrasing the question there lay the implied statement that she would not go to the trouble of preparing it, but would delegate the task to the elderly woman of mixed blood in the flower-print house dress who was conversing in the background with the deck hand, or, worse still, that she phrased it in that way in the hope that they would not accept, thus finding themselves obliged to regard the visit as having ended. Tomatis has apparently thought the same thing since, without consulting anyone, he replied immediately.

"No. It's getting a little late. We ought to be heading back, don't you think so, Pinocchio?"

So after an affable, short, conventional farewell, they started back. They had no sooner walked a few meters down the sandy path toward the water's edge – their shadows, now long, blue, preceded them, breaking up on the irregularities of the ground – when Tomatis, prudently lowering his voice a little, began criticizing Washington's daughter.

"As though the manuscript could be analyzed scientifically in Rincón Norte just as well as in Cambridge! She read the news of his death in the newspaper and now she's playing the part of the devoted daughter. She wants the author to be Washington, no matter what, because, since it's a novel, she thinks she'll make a fortune when it's published. She must already be thinking of selling the film rights, or worse still, of having it adapted for television."

Discreetly, almost stoically, Soldi and Pigeon have forborne to answer those spiteful and doubtless unverifiable remarks, thinking at the same time however that Julia's stubbornness, stemming from confused and probably long-standing emotional struggles, justifies Tomatis's fury to a certain extent.

Then, in silence, they have slowly gone on down toward the river, in the late afternoon heat. Pigeon willingly, or willfully rather, kept glancing all about him, endeavoring to capture in the landscape, rather bleak, moreover, after so many weeks of drought, something, a force peculiar to the disposition of the grayish grass, the dusty vegetation, the sandy soil, the stifling air and the boundless and already slightly pale sky of the dying day, a particular breath that would have been specific to that place and to no other, but his glances ricocheted off this unrecognizable, atonic, neutral space, which brought him, as they say, no feeling of reciprocity and no emotion. Only when they reached the river bank and he had already abandoned the attempt to feel some living intimacy between the compacted folds within his being and the outside, did the proximity and the sight of the water give rise in him to a sort of fleeting happiness that he attributed not to his affinity with that precise river, but to the general alertness of his vitals, of his senses and of his skin, plagued by heat, fatigue and thirst, in the benevolent, immediate and generic presence of the redeeming water.

Since the sun was setting more and more swiftly, they rolled up the green- and white-striped awning of the motorboat so that, thanks to its movement, the air would dry off their sweating faces after the walk and the day just past, which gave the impression of having gone by only for the adults, because the two adolescents, sitting next to each other in the same place on the bench that they had occupied during the trip out, bearing more of a resemblance, one alongside the other, to the two halves of an androgynous being than to two individuals typifying opposite sexes, impassive and relaxed, gave the impression of being, to that which corrodes from within and from without with its insidious and continuous obstinacy, indifferent and invulnerable. Collapsed on the benches, the adults were drinking cold water that they had taken out of the refrigerator, and were allowing themselves to be rocked to and fro by the movement of the boat and by the uniform drone of the motor which, paradoxically, grew fainter in the total silence of the river and of the deserted islands. In the cabin, the deck hand, with his back turned to them, every so often, keeping control of the boat the while and not even turning around, extended his left arm, shouting and pointing toward something on the bank. As he himself must have known that from the stern what he said could not be heard, he gave the impression of pointing it out to himself with an emphatic, peremptory gesture like that of a madman in a critical state, until Soldi rose to his feet and went to ask him what was going on, coming back after a few minutes' affable conversation to explain that those insistent gestures were meant to call the passengers' attention to the giant water lilies floating near the river banks, circular green trays, and alongside each one, at the tip of a long, half-submerged stem that brought an umbilical cord to mind, the white flower with a pink tinge that had opened in the late afternoon, to gleam with a dim splendor during the night and close once again at dawn, until dusk the following day, the victoria regias which the Guaraní Indians called *irupé* and which reminded Pigeon, because of that flower slightly separated from the green circle yet dependent upon it, like a planet and its satellite, of those archaic, solitary goddesses who, fecundating themselves, gave birth between their vigorous limbs to a minor god, white, frail, slender and graceful, with whom they rose in nuptial flight before abandoning him on the sacrificial altar to be hacked to pieces and thus perpetuate their own cult.

As on the trip out, on the trip back too they have slowed down a little, so as to arrive at dusk and thus avoid having to tolerate, amid the stifling-hot houses and pavement, the spongy, blurred late afternoon sun. Making their way down the Colastiné, hugging the eastern bank, skirting the large islands that separate it from the Paraná properly so called and from the river branches skirting Entre Ríos, they have explored the inner canals of the river, formed by the little alluvial islands that until not long before were sandbanks and that do not even have a name, and then, instead of continuing on downriver, they have entered the Ubajay, and even went past, before returning to the mainstream of the Colastiné, the little beach of Rincón and the Garays' weekend house, one of the last properties belonging to the family (now reduced to Pigeon, his wife and their children), the final details of whose sale had in fact been the reason for his trip from Paris. He had not even gone to visit those two houses, shut up and empty for a long time now. A lawyer cousin – as children they detested each other – had taken charge of the sale, and even though Pigeon could have sent him a power of attorney from Paris, he had preferred not to do so in order that the pretext of signing the final papers would serve to justify the journey to the city. On catching sight of the house, not yet in ruins but badly weathered, so that the white of the walls where the paint has not peeled is covered with an archipelago of gray and blackish stains, just as the boat left a tight curve behind, he has again had the hope that something within him, nostalgia, grief, memory, compassion would be set in motion, but, once again, the agglutinated layers of his being, as though they were a single compact block, have refused to come apart, or even open slightly. He has even had to make an effort to point the house out to his son, raising his voice a little over the drone of the motorboat:

"That's the house in Rincón, that I've shown you so many snapshots of. When we were children, we spent our summers here with Cat."

Without answering, the little Frenchman nodded his head, and to please his father, cast a long lingering glance at the house, until another bend in the river hid it from sight, but his impenetrable, serene expression, very similar, Tomatis thought, looking at him, to that of the twins when they were the same age, allowed, despite the intense emotion that he was feeling and that had nothing to do with the house, no outward sign to show. From that house Cat and Elisa had disappeared several years before, leaving, literally, not a trace. They had gone there, as had been their habit for years, to spend a few days together, and no one ever saw them again. The house in Rincón had always been for them the sacrosanct retreat where they periodically repeated the ritual of adultery. The street door was, as usual, unlocked, but everything was still neat and clean. There were no signs of a struggle or of foreign presences. The beds were made and the table set. In the refrigerator, food supplies for several days were still unspoiled. Although there were several valuable objects, a typewriter, electric fans and other devices, nothing was missing and everything was still in its proper place, intact and in perfect working order. A friend in the advertising business, for whom Cat did a bit of work every once in a while, was the one who discovered that they had disappeared: since those were times of terror and violence, and since, on entering the silent house, he began to smell an odor that made him sick to his stomach, the friend in the advertising business became quite frightened, but when he went into the kitchen he discovered that the odor came from a piece of meat that was decomposing on the counter, on a plate. Alongside it was a large kitchen knife and a butcher board, but there had not been time to use them. At precisely the moment that the plate of meat had been taken out of the refrigerator and set down on the red tiles of the counter, the flow of their acts had stopped and they had, as the saying goes, disappeared into thin air. In seven or eight years not one sign of their material existence, or even their remains, had ever again appeared. *They went,* Tomatis had remarked to Pigeon in a letter, *from an undeserved bed to an undeserved grave, with that discreet and mutually supportive autonomy, their backs to the world and even opposed to it, granted only by mysticism, madness and adultery.*

The motor launch left the Ubajay – "It's nearly as wide as the Seine at the Pont des Arts and around here everyone calls it a little stream," Pigeon thought as they gradually left it behind – and entered the Colastiné once again, heading due south. In the hot, motionless late March afternoon, because of the slightly cooler air resulting from its movement, *Blondie* gave Pigeon the impression of passing through a corridor different from the rest of space, with a climate all its own, milder than the one that reigned beyond its boundaries and seeming to dissolve the low-lying, colorless islands in the murky air. They were now navigating down a real river, broad, deep and swift-flowing, even though its surface was smooth – owing to the weather and the hour – and nearly coagulated, like a block of gelatin in which the slender prow of the launch kept opening a furrow which widened out at the stern and in which the masses of water hollowed out had the consistency, the color and the texture of rough veining, and, because of the seething white bubbles that formed on the surface, of furiously boiling caramel. And as a river, so real, Pigeon has remembered, that, despite being no more than a meander, an excrescence, a side stream among so many others that the Paraná forms as it flows southward, on its banks, some ten kilometers farther downriver, in Colastiné Sur, until the 20s more or less, where the city port was located, there had once been a seaport, and in its environs, now deserted and returned to the wild state, there had been a teeming multitude of Russian, Japanese, German, Senegalese, Australian sailors, tradesmen, river functionaries and stevedores, prostitutes and smugglers, craftsmen and officials and agents of the army and the port police. From Dakar, Hamburg, Odessa or New England, ships with tall prows, masts and smokestacks, anchored along the shore. A train came out from the city, crossing the lagoon via a wooden bridge that, like nearly all the others, was eventually destroyed by a flood, unloading and loading freight and passengers. Docks and warehouses extended all down the shore with railway tracks running through the space that separated them, and a tumult of carts, horses, men, winches hustled and bustled, amid piles of wood and bales of white cloth which, having been brought up from the dark holds of the ships in which they had crossed more than one ocean, were piled up, waiting in the sun on the sandy ground for the freight cars to take them into the city. The town properly so called had consisted of a number of straight rows of little houses with zinc roofs, one or another of them, more pretentious, adorned with a tin eave representing a fleur de lys or some other motif, repeated all along the facade, at the top, parallel to the zinc rain gutter. Like mosquitoes and flies around men, the minuscule patched boats, propelled by sail, oar, or motor, of suppliers, tradesmen, functionaries and even panders, pestered, moving, unstable and nervous, round about them, the large oceangoing vessels, motionless and firmly at anchor alongside the dock. The dredging of the new port, in the city, and the construction of the long canal affording access to the docks from an intricate knot of islands, rivers, rivulets, lagoons and small streams that flowed into the Paraná Viejo, contributed to the decline of the port in Colastiné Sur. The town and the railroad station disappeared; the docks and warehouses, little by little, fell to pieces; grass and weeds gradually grew over the roads that led to the port: there remained a grove of eucalyptus, a small bar made of sheets of tin and wood from crates, with a straw roof, and here and there, all along the shore as far as Rincón, several stretches of railway track, rusted and buried under faded vegetation, good iron ingots that, for some mysterious reason, junk men, collectors of building materials or mere thieves, had refrained from tearing up. Also, incomplete and partially broken apart by the pressure exerted from below by what keeps stubbornly expanding, the rectangular bases of the little wooden houses which, in the era of fat kine, had been afforded the luxury of a cement foundation. But from a certain distance, from the river or from the middle of the countryside, for example, the vestiges of human occupation are of course invisible, except for the corrugated tin shack, the eucalyptus and the geometric black pilings, reminiscent of certain drawings by Piranesi, of a recent dock set aside for a military barge that transports fuel trucks, the spot seems as virgin and uninhabited as it must have been, apart from the climate, the erosion and the alluvial deposits, on the day when, after the last geological upheaval, the soil, the water, the air and the vegetation, each gradually finding its place, settled down.

While Pigeon imagined its being possible to make use of the Soldi family's various means of transportation, he never dared hope for so much, and the journey they have taken this afternoon to Rincón Norte with Tomatis and the youngsters will doubtless remain with him as one of the best moments of his stay, although his impressions and even his sensations have been rather neutral, distant and slightly unreal. Therefore, when *Blondie* has begun to make its way down the Colastiné, after leaving behind that "little stream," the Ubajay, he has taken it upon himself to converse a bit with Pinocchio, questioning him about the dactylogram. Minutely, calmly, punctiliously, employing precise, well-rounded phrases, for some ten minutes during which Pigeon and Tomatis have listened attentively, almost overcome with astonishment, Pinocchio has summed up the main plot lines of the story, and in the air altered by the movement of the launch, the old legendary names, Troy, Helen, Paris, Menelaus, Agamemnon and Ulysses, and above all the Old Soldier and the Young Soldier – the two-part singing voice of the story according to Pinocchio – have hovered for a moment after having been uttered, to be carried off almost immediately like bits of paper or like dead leaves by the moving air. Pigeon has followed the oral summary of the story with shakes of his head, and Pinocchio's precise and elaborate phrases seem to have made more and more distant, if not nonexistent, the continuous drone – which is an illusion – of the motor. Then

Pinocchio has said that he is drafting a written resumé, some fifty pages long, to send to universities, critics, publishers, as soon as Washington's daughter gives him permission to take the original out of the house and have it photocopied. He is, Pinocchio has said, prepared to type the whole thing, if Julia allows him to. Then he has fallen silent, looking thoughtfully at the deck hand who, with his back to his passengers, appears not to be steering the helm but to have leaned on it to rest from the fatigue of the torrid day. At one point they have sailed underneath the highway bridge of Verduc Island, and have seen the ribbon of asphalt that leads, straight and blue, to the tunnel underneath the river at the other end of the island, to Paraná, and even to Uruguay and Brazil, and have arrived at the place where the Colastiné River ends, its waters mingling with the two smaller Tiradero streams, the old and the new, which in turn flow together to form such intricate water courses – ephemeral or permanent, large or small, shallow or deep, wide or narrow, following the caprice of low water levels and high – that they do not even have a name. Abandoning its southerly heading, the launch veered off westward and entered the Santa Fe River, a narrow watercourse whose depth alone, perhaps, allowed it to be called a river, and so tortuous that, as was being demonstrated by the position on the horizon of the last large red splotches of the later afternoon, which continually changed place, it obliged them to take first an easterly heading, then northeasterly, then southeasterly, then easterly, then southeasterly, then northeasterly, then southerly, then westerly and finally, in the place called the Vuelta del Paraguayo, to take an east-southeast heading, and after that again to take, and this time keep to, a heading due west, that is to say toward the city.

The last red light of the now invisible sun was darkening the silhouettes of the buildings; the tallest constructions, high-rises, chimneys, grain elevators at the port, gave Pigeon the impression of being plane geometrical figures, black and without depth, and the multitude of low houses, one or two stories high, plus the tops of the trees, a dark mass, with no particular reliefs and an irregular perimeter that followed the silhouette of the whole along its highest edge, as though it had been that of an elongated black tumulus. But that dark background, which seemed to be cut out of rigid cardboard, carefully coated with India ink, was not large enough to cover the enormous patch of red light against which it loomed up. The light, which in its stubborn expansion, ought on encountering that obstacle to have impatiently piled up against its reverse side, poured over the edges of the black silhouette, making them sparkle, and then scattered, freed though a little exhausted now, throughout space, so that the launch was sailing not on the river of dusk, but in a solemn, strange reddish semidarkness. Launch, water, vegetation seemed made of one and the same substance, of a dark reddish cast and somewhat phosphorescent – a single flow of matter assuming, for a few moments still, many different concrete forms which the darkness was preparing to even out. Raising his voice so as to be heard above the drone of the motor, in a manner at once brusque and calm, Tomatis began to recite:

> *O frati, dissi, che per cento milia*
> *perigli siete giunti a l'occidente,*
> *a questa tanto picciola vigilia*
> *d'i nostri sensi ch'è del remanente*

non vogliate negar l'esperienza,
di retro al sol, del mondo sanza gente.
Considerate la vostra semenza;
fatti nos foste a viver come bruti
ma per seguir virtute e canoscenza.

When he finished, Tomatis voiced a discreet and pleased exclamation, and silence again set in. There remained the drone of the launch which, in the proximity of the Yacht Club, seeking an empty place to land amid the craft anchored along the shore, began to slow down. The stream empties, at the club, into the broad expanse of water that, precisely because of its breadth, the inhabitants of the region and even the maps call the lagoon, at which, abruptly, the city comes to an end, after six or seven kilometers of coastal roads, beaches, bridges still standing or destroyed by time or the current, boat clubs, port seawalls, warehouses, ring roads, slums: a teeming anthill along the edge of the flat, monotonous labyrinth of islands and water, islands and water. The broad expanse of the lagoon, beyond which practically speaking the countryside begins with no outskirts of the city as a transition, forms a large empty space above water, so that when the launch had to go on, accelerating a bit, to the center of the lagoon so as to turn around more easily and go back to the club dock where the deck hand had in all likelihood spied an empty spot in which to tie up, Pigeon noted that the reddish tinge had disappeared from things and that night had now fallen at last: a night at the end of summer, like so many others that he had entered over so many years, where there palpitated, more than in the busy, noisy daytime, the anonymous and archaic presences of the vegetation, the water, the uncultivated open country that surrounded the city, of the terrestrial, aquatic and aerial fauna that crawled over the sandy soil, swam in the silence and darkness of the river bottoms, swarmed in the swamps, glided, cautiously and cruelly, on their nocturnal expeditions across the countryside and the islands, making the grass, the air, the branches rustle. Raising his head, Pigeon has been able to see, in a sky still bright, where the last violet traces had given way beneath the generalized blue, the first stars. In an instantaneous flash – the sound of the water, more distinct than during the boat trip because the motor had stopped, revealing the quiet of the night, no doubt contributed to his sudden clairvoyance – he has understood why, despite his good will, his efforts even, since his arrival from Paris after so many years of absence, his birthplace has produced no emotion in him: because he is at last an adult, and to be an adult means, precisely, having reached the point of understanding that it is not in one's native land that one has been born, but in a larger, more neutral place, neither friend nor enemy, unknown, which no one could call his own and which does not give rise to affection but, rather, to strangeness, a home that is not spatial or geographical, or even verbal, but rather, and insofar as those words can continue to mean something, physical, chemical, biological, cosmic, and of which the invisible and the visible, from one's fingertips to the starry universe, or what can ultimately be known about the invisible and the visible, form a part, and that that whole which includes even the very limits of the inconceivable, is not in reality his homeland but his prison, itself abandoned and locked from the outside – the boundless darkness that wanders, at once glacial and igneous, beyond the reach not only of the senses, but also of emotion, of nostalgia and of thought.

Morvan was, as I was telling you, looking out through the window at the darkness that there, in December, around Christmas, comes on swiftly, when, after knocking determinedly on the door and without giving him time to answer, his three principal collaborators, Captain Lautret and Inspectors Combes and Juin entered the office. Generally impenetrable and opaque to strangers, most individuals are usually transparent to their peers, at least as regards their immediate intentions, so that before his visitors opened their mouths, Morvan realized that they had lunched together and had agreed on what they were going to discuss with him, and what they were going to discuss with him, with Lautret taking the lead, had, Morvan knew, to do with the letter that had arrived recently not from the permanent headquarters of the Crime Squad, nor from the office of the Chief of Police, nor from that of the Paris Prefect, but directly from the Ministry. With the aim of circulating it among the police officers of the Special Bureau, Morvan had given the letter to Lautret to have photocopies of it made and distribute them, but when the police officers halted, standing near the window, he noted that the sheet of paper, folded in four, that Lautret took out of his pocket, was not a photocopy but the original that he had given him. Once its bureaucratic euphemisms had been deciphered and summed up in a few words, the letter from the Ministry said more or less that after nine months of massacres, of incomprehensible attitudes, of useless expenditures and of bad publicity, mentioned in that order, it was evident that the results were nonexistent, so that there could be expected, in an immediate future, but this was said in a deliberately vague and veiled manner, a series of reforms, transfers and disciplinary actions.

Lautret unfolded the letter and held it in the air for a moment, without reading it, without handing it to anyone, without even looking at it or making any comment regarding its contents. The four men remained motionless and silent, facing each other, standing near the window, in Morvan's lighted office in which, because of his excessive predilection for order, not a speck of dust was floating about, there was not a single piece of paper in the ashtray or in the unused wastebasket next to his chair, or the slightest trace of crushed ashes in the bottom of the ashtray. Without resembling each other physically, and despite slight differences in age, the four men were nonetheless similar, and their common features, while owed to their dress and the automatisms of their profession, also stemmed from the era and the civilization to which they belonged. Solidly built and purely exterior, in the prime of life, transparent, as I was saying, to each other insofar as daily conventions were concerned, but deaf and blind to the impenetrable depths in which the ephemeral days that civilizations endure are rooted. The heavy winter garments that gave them a supplementary bulkiness, doubtless purchased in the same shops, must have cost more or less the same, and if Captain Lautret's gave the impression of being a little more expensive and just a bit flashier, the difference came only from a higher note on the same scale of costs and tastes. The nuances of temperament they displayed no more defined each of them than the different forms that the foliage of plants of a single species may assume. At once strange and familiar, they were nonetheless more sensitive to what was familiar than to what was strange in each of them. And their conflicts with the world in which they had grown up were all of a superficial nature, since at no time, not even in the troubled years of adolescence, had they ever ceased to think and to feel that the order of that world was immutable. They took it for granted that they belonged to a certain civilization, and that fact was to them indisputable, like geological formations or the circulation of the blood, and if someone had told them that the illiterate African who, abandoning his tribe, endeavors to enter in secret, after weeks of privation in the dark belly of a ship, one or another of the countries that are said to belong to that civilization, is more European than millions and millions of Europeans, they would have felt, and I do not doubt their sincerity for a moment, puzzled or indignant. Having been molded for centuries to consider themselves as the clear nucleus of the world, all of their aberrations were dismissed when they formulated their own essence, which, naturally, they neglected to do when they defined that of others. The four of them respected technical skill, professional success, physical dexterity and were practitioners of corporate solidarity, moral relativism and weekends in the country. And if Morvan, or anyone else, owing to his personal characteristics, strayed from these norms, he did so only from a practical point of view, because deep within himself they continued to appear to him to be the natural laws of existence.

"He ought to be nicer to those who have been offering him hospitality for twenty years," Tomatis says. "Don't you think so, Pinocchio?"

"I haven't yet formed an opinion on that score," Soldi says.

Pigeon breaks off his story, but it is evident that he has not considered Tomatis's comment to be of the slightest importance; indeed, it is as though he hadn't heard it, and from his expression, the others understand that his silence of several seconds has no object other than that of allowing him to concentrate even more on the details of what he is recounting, because he closes his eyes slightly and tosses his head back, so that his bald spot, his forehead, the tip of his nose and his chin covered with blond stubble, which has again appeared despite his having taken particular care when shaving that morning, shine, still damp, on being exposed in a more direct way to certain of the lights in the patio, attached to the top of a white wall near the kitchen quarters, or hanging in garlands amid the branches of the giant acacias or between the trunks of the palm trees. Since before going on Pigeon stirs a bit so as to be more comfortably seated in his chair, when he changes the position of his legs, the soles of his moccasins scrape against the reddish powdered brick underfoot. As the patio, which occupies one whole street corner, is quite large, separated from the sidewalk by a row of balustrades painted white, there is a great deal of space between the tables, and as there is no breeze at all, the enormous tops of the acacias and the sharp-edged, curved leaves of the palms, because of the electric bulbs illuminating them from several directions at once, creating alternate zones of light and dark, gleam like flakes of mica, giving the impression of belonging to a kingdom all their own, an inconceivable cross between the vegetable and the mineral. To Pigeon's left, beyond the little white row of balustrades, on the far side of the dark street, is the long bus terminal, in which the hustle and bustle, since it is already almost ten, has died down a little because of the time of night. At the far end of the patio, beyond the tables placed here and there beneath the trees, at the foot of the tall white wall, there is a combination bar, small kitchen and grill, strictly speaking a long shed of whitewashed brick, with the lateral walls and two partitions between them making three rooms that are independent but joined by a common roof made of straw. Three or four waiters are walking, with loaded trays, down the powdered brick paths that lead to the tables that are occupied. That is what he, Pigeon, sees, over and on either side of Tomatis's shoulders at this moment: a sort of border or moving, lighted background adorning Tomatis's torso, slightly hazier than the objects close to hand, like a photo-graphic slide shown on a screen. His tanned skin and dark blue shirt, as well as his still stubbornly black, tousled hair plastered to his temples with sweat, seem even darker in contrast to the bright moving décor against which they stand out. Tomatis, however, in the chair opposite, with his back to the center of the patio, can see, behind Pigeon's bald spot and yellow shirt, the less well-lighted corners of the outdoor area. Tomatis perceives, on the other side of the trees, the side street that forms the corner, beyond the little lateral enclosure of white balustrades. To have more peace and quiet, they have chosen the last table, so that the motionless background, almost in semidarkness, against which Pigeon's torso is outlined emphasizes and brings out the color of his light, almost golden, tan, characteristic of that taken on by the skin of certain blonds, and at any event, Tomatis thinks, identical to Cat's, and his yellow shirt. To give the patio a touch of local, or more precisely, national color, a series of cart wheels, painted white and held upright by supports of white bricks, are set out in a line, approximately a meter apart, all along the perimeter of the patio, except on the side occupied by the kitchen quarters, parallel to the little white balustraded enclosure. The wrought iron tables and chairs are white too. And overhead, amid the garlands of lights that really light the patio, there can be seen other garlands of little colored bulbs which, suspended among the leaves, seem like a rather charmless imitation of real yellow acacia flowers, which have bloomed, faded, fallen, decayed, dried out and turned to dust almost half a year ago by now.

Occupying the corner of the table, Soldi has Pigeon to his left and Tomatis to his right, so that, beyond a couple of cart wheels painted white and the little low white row of balustrades, and beyond the dark street, he can see the low, well-lighted bus terminal. Every so often, an interurban bus or a black and yellow taxi goes slowly up or down the dark street, entering or leaving the terminal, and disappears in the empty, sultry darkness. The first three glasses of beer – wine has seemed inappropriate to them on such a hot night – that the waiter has just served, and from which the three have immediately taken a long swallow, are sitting half-empty among the little dishes of appetizers, peanuts in the shell, lupin seeds, little cubes of cheese and mortadella. Several seconds after having been poured into their tenebrous entrails, the beer has seemed to want to make its escape again, in the form of great drops of sweat that have suddenly appeared on their foreheads and necks, sliding down amid the burning-hot folds of their skin. Soldi can feel that his beard is damp and matted. Despite the fact that the three of them are together, sitting at the same table, because of the different position that they are each occupying at it, perhaps later on, when the night that they are sharing comes to mind again, they will not have the same memories. It is evident that, with regard to Pigeon's story too, each of them will have a different view, not only Soldi and Tomatis, but Pigeon in particular, who will never be able to verify the exact tenor of his words in the imagination of the others. But in any case, having given the ironic comments of his listeners (Soldi's having perhaps been provoked by Tomatis's question) a few seconds' time to dissipate in the warm air, half closing his eyes and tossing his head back, Pigeon shakes his hand enigmatically above his half-empty glass of beer and goes on:

Not making a single gesture, Morvan waited for Lautret to make up his mind to speak. In all truth, he had already guessed what he was preparing himself to hear, but in order to calm his collaborators and give them the feeling that the four of them formed a united and efficient team he feigned immense interest. The role that Lautret had been playing, of spokesman for the bureau to the press and the public, was prolonged at that moment within the confines of the office, and Morvan was amused by the official air that Lautret, his lifelong friend, had just adopted to tell him what he himself thought of the letter from the ministry: that only bureaucrats far removed from the field of operations are sufficiently inexperienced and obtuse to believe that suggestions and threats can change the course of events. Lautret's role as spokesman was partially justified, since even though it was likely that they thought the same thing he did, Combes and Juin would never have dared to voice a contrary opinion in Morvan's presence. As well as the respect that they had for the Captain there was an added factor, a sort of conformism whereby, even though they did not believe in the pertinence of threats, they took them literally because they came from their superiors. To put it another way, knowing that they themselves and everyone in the Special Bureau had been working without a break, day and night, for nine months now, unable to show their discontent except by way of Lautret's reaction, they held fairness in less esteem than hierarchy. There was also something histrionic in Lautret's attitude, in the excessive formality of his protests since, in view of the friendship that, as they say, united them, he could have come to Morvan to speak of the problem in a more informal way, and Morvan began to wonder whether, having taken the letter from the Ministry more seriously than he admitted, Lautret, adopting the view that transfers and sanctions in the Special Bureau were inevitable, was not already preparing, by assuming leadership over his subordinates, to take the place of the head of the bureau. It must not be forgotten that, as official spokesman, Lautret was, to the press and the public, more of a celebrity than Morvan, who worked, more by temperament than by being obliged to do so, in a discreet semidarkness. But that suspicion, which left him indifferent, and not only because deep within himself he placed no credence in it, disappeared immediately when, without the slightest transition, Lautret abandoned his supposed indignation, let out a belly laugh, and before the puzzled eyes of his three interlocutors, began to tear, slowly and relentlessly, the letter from the Ministry to, as they say, bits.

Despite his broad, heartfelt, amused laughter, which made him shake all over, they perceived something impenetrable in his suddenly unfamiliar face, and since, as the pieces gradually grew smaller and smaller, the increasing thickness of the paper he still had left to tear made it more resistant, Lautret's unjustified and excessive guffaw turned into jerky grimaces from the effort demanded of him by what he was doing. Without losing his composure, Morvan studied him, less scandalized than on the alert. Despite his spontaneous burst of laughter, Lautret's disproportionate and above all sudden violence, revealing a sort of incongruity, aroused an intrigued curiosity in the bureau chief, which in his case was a sort of instinct or a reflex, and was what had led him to become a police officer. Lautret had accustomed him to violence and even brutality, but he had always considered the use that his friend made of them to be a technique aimed at obtaining precise results and one in which, so to speak, only the police officer was present, with no participation of the person. The two inspectors gave the impression that they were regretting this visit to the bureau chief's office, so that Morvan, to reassure them, making an effort to overcome his own perplexity, began to smile, shaking his head. At precisely that moment Lautret, with a quick and efficient gesture, threw all the little bits of paper in the air, over the heads of his colleagues. A slow rain of little white papers, scattering in the air after Lautret's energetic launch, began to drift downward in the lighted room, and since many little bits turned round and round as they allowed themselves to be attracted, without excessive haste, owing to their small weight, by the force of gravity, the empty space between the four men standing face to face became full of a silent white agitation, something inconsistent with the psychological tension that was perceptible in Morvan's office, as he, without knowing why, gazed as though bewitched at the delicate, soundless whirlwind, slowly turned his head toward the window and saw first the little white papers reflected in the frosty windowpanes, and when he concentrated harder on what he was seeing, even though in the beginning he found it difficult to believe, he discovered to his astonishment that beyond the windowpanes, amid the bare branches of the plane trees, and all through the freezing blue air of the winter dusk, the rain of little white papers had become general, and after just a fraction of a second of confusion, during which he might well have traversed a magic universe, he realized that it was snowing outside.

When the others left the office, Morvan stayed for a while watching the snow fall, until it was pitch dark and the flakes that were falling, at times obliquely and serenely and at times in furious whorls, became, because of the contrast with the darkness, brighter and whiter. Despite the fact that many bars and shops were still lighted, there was almost no one on the streets now. Although the last god of the West was incarnated, as they say, in this world and crucified at the age of thirty-three, in order that the big stores, the supermarkets and the gift shops might increase their sales volume on his birthday, his worshipers, who have replaced prayer by purchase on credit and the veneration of martyrs by the autographed photo of a soccer player, who hope for no miracles other than a trip for two won in the lottery of a television game, had deserted because of the bad weather the only places of worship that they frequent regularly and without the slightest trace of hypocrisy: shopping centers. Gazing at the dark, deserted streets, the snow falling in whorls forming an iridescent halo around the street lamps, Morvan had a presentiment that the shadow that he had been chasing for nine months now, impossible to catch despite his alarming proximity, was starting to move again, determined to strike.

Before leaving, he picked up, patiently and meticulously, all the bits of white paper and put them in a metal ashtray that had never been used. Since they had scattered all over the room, because of their lightness perhaps and, it occurred to him, the expectant breathing of the four police officers that disturbed, as it speeded up, without their realizing it, the ambient air, he had to crawl about the office a little so as to pick them all up, underneath the desk or the chairs, two or three inexplicably at the other end of the room and even three or four that had fallen into the empty wastebasket without one piece of paper in it, so free of dust, or of any other dirt, that he could have cooked in it. Once he had finished piling them up in the ashtray, and after taking a last look around the room to make sure that he had not left a single one still to be picked up, he stood there lost in thought for a moment, ashtray in hand, until finally, instead of putting it back on top of the desk, he opened a metal locker and placed it inside. Then he put on his overcoat, hat and gloves, and went out into the street.

Although it was rather late by now, many shops were still open because of the holidays, and although there were still many cars on the boulevard, the snow deadened all sounds. Only the creaking of his shoes against the layer of snow that was becoming thicker and thicker on the sidewalk, accompanied, rhythmically, Morvan's footsteps. Heading first toward the Place León Blum, he walked all the way around it, peeking discreetly, without stopping, inside the bars and the lighted shops, most of them half empty or altogether so. In the Burger King, as it was rather late by now, the clientele of children and adolescents had disappeared, but two or three adults, alone and rushed for time, were removing French fries from a cardboard carton with their fingers and raising them distractedly to their mouths. In Le Relais du XI, the chairs had already been placed on the tables and an employee of the bar was sweeping the place out. Morvan felt the snow landing on his hat, penetrating the cloth of his overcoat at the shoulders. If he raised his head, his face was riddled with sharp, cold pricks. He walked on, all hunched over, amid the white whorls of snowflakes that the wind tore at, giving them many different forms, sizes and consistencies, from the soft, classic little ball like a handful of cotton wool, through drops and even slivers of snow so hard and gleaming that it was already ice, to a fine white powder that drifted about amid the flakes and made one's breath dusty, penetrating to one's lungs like a little cloud of ice-cold cocaine. Morvan crossed the Rue de la Roquette and headed for the supermarket, stopping at the entrance and contemplating the place through the display windows. The private watchman, who knew him, standing inside near the entrance, gave him a friendly wave of his hand. Morvan answered with a nod of his head. In the long row of cashiers' stations, several were already closed, but at the ones that were still open a number of customers were standing in line waiting their turn to pay for the merchandise that filled the metal shopping carts or red plastic baskets belonging to the supermarket. At one of the cash registers, an elderly, well-dressed woman, with two bottles of champagne in her arms, was waiting in line behind a young man with a blond beard who was paying for his purchases. Morvan stood hesitating on the sidewalk for a moment, but after giving another nod in the watchman's direction, he went on his way.

He walked a little way down the Avenue Parmentier, and turning down the Rue Sedaine, passed by the municipal building, crossed the Boulevard Voltaire, and entered the short narrow streets, many of them dead ends, that lead away on either side of the Rue de la Roquette, the Rue Sedaine and other long streets, busy during the daytime, such as the Rue de Charonne or the Rue du Chemin Vert, which, cutting across the Boulevard Voltaire, lead from the Père Lachaise cemetery to the Bastille. As he entered the dark, the silence grew, the lights of the shops and even those of apartments gradually went out, and the snow grew thicker, muffling even the sound of his footsteps in the dark, unreal streets of the ghostly city. The garbage sacks, of black or blue plastic, piled up along the sidewalks, were turning as rigid as corpses and the snow that was falling accumulated in their folds and hollows. Despite the raised lapels of his overcoat, Morvan felt the powdered snow penetrating his nostrils and the icy air freezing his ears, his forehead and the tip of his nose. The cold made him sleepy or, rather, seemed to put a greater and greater distance between him and things. Gradually, the deserted city began to resemble the one in his dream. The dense snow shrank the circle of the visible, and what was left of the city floating round about him seemed to emerge from a thick grayish mist that blended with the blackness. The

turbulent curtain of snow that was falling gave the impression
of deepening the silence, a paradoxical one since on being
confronted with the white elements that are falling, our sense
of sight prepares us, as with rain or hail, not for the
unaccustomed absence of sound but, rather, for a great racket.
For quite some time, and despite his familiarity with them
owing to the frequent patrols that he had been making for
months, he went down dark streets that he had no idea how
to get to the end of and that he was unable to recognize.
Despite the cold, he walked for so long a time through the
deserted city that at a certain moment he began to be aware
of a sense of warmth, and even of a few drops of perspiration
that broke out on the nape of his neck and trickled down his
collar. The imminence of something terrible agitated him –
not of a crime but of a revelation, something of which he had
had a presentiment for months but which he had not dared
to formulate in any clear way out of fear perhaps that that
formulation, given the horror of its meaning, by taking from
him the last traces of hope, would cast him into the ultimate
depths of darkness. He went on walking for hours, and in the
same way as when he engaged in certain sports to excess,
after a while he entered a sort of trance, an enduring
suspension of consciousness which had its agreeable side but
which separated him from the world of the waking state and
kept him from recognizing things familiar to him. Because,
perhaps, of the contrast between the temperature of his body
and the freezing air outside him, at a certain moment he
began to feel shivers – he frequently had that sensation – and
since he saw shining at the corner in the distance the green
neon cross of a pharmacy, past which the snowflakes were
falling, obliquely, he quickened his pace and walked on in

that direction, with the intention of buying a tube of aspirins. The pharmacy was empty, and the pharmacist, looking drowsy, came out of the back of the store and waited on him almost without a word, but when he handed him his change, Morvan noted that the bills had the image of the Gorgon, framed in the oval of a puerile garland, printed on them. He felt like turning around to say something to the pharmacist, but changed his mind and, shrugging his shoulders, gave a little sarcastic laugh to draw attention to how absurd this homage seemed to him. As he left the pharmacy and began putting the change in his wallet, he took out the bills that were in it and perceived that in them as well, Scylla and Charybdis, the Gorgon, the Chimera in the largest ones, were shown surrounded by the unspeakable oval garland. Beneath the blinking green neon cross, that imparted a pale green tinge to the snowflakes around it, like clots of chlorine, Morvan realized that, in some incomprehensible way, without knowing exactly how or when, owing to his having walked in the snow for so long a time, he had passed over into the other world, in which things, without being all that different from those of the waking state, were yet no longer the same and gave rise in him to an increasing uneasiness, quite similar to anxiety. Everything was larger, more silent, more distant. It was still snowing, but the snow was gray. In a little public square in which he suddenly found himself, not knowing how he had gotten there, he came upon one of those strange monuments, with regard to which he was unable to say whether the ambiguity of what they represented was deliberate or, because of the great age of the stone, the result of erosion: giant human being, winged monster, centaur, octopus, equestrian figure or mammoth. It could have been a religious monument, since in this nameless territory it was perhaps the god of the undifferentiated that was worshiped. More puzzled than terrified, he went on his way, slowly walking through the curtain of gray snow, when all of a sudden, somewhere in the immense empty city, a series of blows, insistent and distant, began to be heard. He stopped for a moment in order to determine more precisely the place that they were coming from, and when it seemed to him that he had located it he headed in that direction, which must have been the right one because the blows were growing louder and louder, until, when they sounded very close at hand, he could hear a peremptory voice calling out to him: *Captain! Captain!*

He opened his eyes. His head ached. You will have guessed that the blows were knocks on the door, and that he was being abruptly awakened from a dream. He had slept, as he was in the habit of doing every so often, in one of the little rooms in the Special Bureau set aside for the personnel on night duty to rest in. The room had the very modest dimensions and the lack of everything superfluous that matched Morvan's austere temperament perfectly: a sofa, a little night table, an armchair, a table, a locker and a couple of straight-backed chairs. It overlooked a back lot, narrow and hemmed in by tall blind walls, of gray stone blackened by the elements. Turning on the lamp on the night table, Morvan sat down on the bed and realized that he had gone to sleep with his clothes on, with the exception of his suit coat, but with his sweater and pants and even his shoes on, which did not greatly surprise him, because he knew that on occasion that happened, especially when he slept in the Special Bureau — those times in which an uneasy feeling of imminence came over him, as on the day before, when, after returning from lunch, gazing through the cold windowpanes of his office at the bare branches of the plane trees, he had been certain that the shadow he had been chasing for so many months, close at hand but impossible to catch, emerging from its dark, secret attic, driven by its deadly repetitive impulse, like an endless saw set in motion since the beginning of time, was preparing to strike.

The person who was insistently knocking at the door was an agent on duty who had received an emergency phone call: the concierge of a building on the Rue de la Folie Regnault, worried because the elderly lady whom she was to accompany to the hospital that morning for a medical consultation answered neither the doorbell nor the telephone, was asking that a police officer be dispatched so as to open the woman's door, because, by herself and on her own responsibility, she didn't dare enter the apartment. Morvan looked at his wristwatch, and even though it said 7:10, when he opened the blue curtains over the window, he saw that it was still pitch dark. On all the ledges set into the walls, on what he could manage to see of the rooftops and on the ground in the little back lot, and likewise on the windowsill, the white snow, altogether real, had accumulated, radiating a crystalline light in the black December morning.

His only breakfast was the glass of water in which he dissolved the effervescent aspirin tablet, putting the tube back into the pocket of his overcoat in case he had a long stay ahead of him in the apartment that they were going to inspect. When the agent in the seat alongside him who was driving wanted to turn on the siren, Morvan dissuaded him with a wordless gesture. The snow covered the sidewalks, the little public squares, the cornices, the bare branches of the trees from which long, sharp icicles hung like glass knives. In the street, inasmuch as there had been heavy traffic since early in the day, furrows of dirty snow had been plowed, arousing in Morvan intimate recent associations, without his realizing that those associations came to mind because of the likeness between the dirty snow of the street and the gray flakes of his dream. The concierge was awaiting their arrival with obvious anxiety, keeping a close watch from her room on the ground floor. Though she must have been around fifty, and owing to a hard life looked a little older, on seeing her behind the windowpane, her inordinately wide-open eyes, her obviously dyed, still disheveled black hair that the shock so early in the morning had not given her time to arrange properly, her heavyset matron's body wrapped in a padded bathrobe, Morvan calculated with terrible accuracy and with relief as well that, if her fate depended on the man, or whatever it was, that took such pleasure in hacking elderly ladies to pieces, she had a lot of time ahead of her, since, as experience proved, she still looked too young to be tortured. Just as he and the agent reached the entrance, they heard the sound of the electric buzzer, and pushing open the heavy hand-carved door with bronze handles – the building had not lost its standing during its existence of almost a century – they entered the dark vestibule, where the concierge was already waiting for them, keys in hand.

They climbed the stairs to the fourth floor, and panting, waited for the concierge to open, with some difficulty, the door, with a double turn of the key to undo the bolt. Without entering the apartment, Morvan stretched his arm out to one side, feeling along the inside wall next to the door, searching for the light switch, and once he had found the angular protuberance, he pressed it with the tip of his index finger, turning on the light in the vestibule. It was a small entry hall with a mirror, a coat rack and narrow little table with turned legs standing against the wall below the mirror. A light green wall-to-wall carpet, no doubt frequently gone over with a minute vacuum cleaner, covered the floor of this very limited space, and probably that of the entire apartment, except for the bathroom and the kitchen. Without moving from the doorway, Morvan inspected the vestibule, while the agent and the concierge tried to look over his shoulder to see inside.

"Look," Morvan said to the agent, stepping aside to point something out to him: halfway between the closed door opposite, which led to the rooms inside, and the open doorway in which the two were standing, practically in the center of the tiny vestibule, on the floor, standing out against the bright green carpeting, was a little piece of white paper, no bigger than a twenty-centime piece.

I am certain that the agent attributed Morvan's sudden and quite unusual paleness to the fact that the police captain had gone to bed late, long after midnight – the agent knew this because he had gone back on duty at twelve and had seen him enter the Special Bureau quite a while after that, with his usual absent expression, at once amiable and distant, his hat and the shoulders of his overcoat covered with snow. But his attention must also have been attracted by the fact that, for a goodly number of seconds, the captain's eyes were riveted on the little piece of paper, with his head slightly tilted toward his left shoulder, as he stood there staring at it, seemingly fascinated. Then he turned to the policeman and the concierge and said, in an official, almost solemn tone of voice, as though taking them as witnesses:

"We are now proceeding to enter the apartment."

And crossing the threshold, he entered the tiny vestibule and kneeled down on the floor, his eyes not leaving for a single moment the bit of white paper that stood out against the bright green carpeting. He took out of his wallet a little transparent plastic envelope, the size of a pack of cigarettes – he kept several of them, carefully folded, in one compartment of his wallet – and pressing the stiff edges of the upper portion with his fingers to spread them apart, held the opening of the little envelope on top of the carpet a few millimeters away from the little white paper. Then, with the gloved index finger of his other hand, he pushed the bit of paper toward the inside of the envelope till it slid in, so that by ceasing to press down on the stiff edges of the opening with the index finger and the thumb of his left hand, he caused the opening to close by itself, and shaking his gloved hand so that the little piece of paper would slip down to the bottom of the envelope, when he decided that it was safely inside, he put the envelope in his pocket. Then he stepped forward a few paces, opened the door that led inside the apartment, took a look about, and turning around, told the concierge to go downstairs to her little room on the ground floor and not to budge from there. Without yet having seen what was inside, the policeman realized that a hard day had begun for the Special Bureau and that since he had been on duty all night long, he, luckily, would soon be relieved.

In contrast to the little entryway, in the living room there reigned a disorder that, to be precise, I would be obliged to describe as fierce. Chance can be devastating, but it is never methodical or meticulous. And although it is true that, from a certain point of view, everything having to do with human acts is madness, it would be prudent to reserve that word to designate something specific and not beyond reason, but the result of a reason all its own that orders the world according to a system of meanings that are without a flaw and on precisely that account impenetrable from the outside. Morvan knew that the stage set that the room had been turned into had a meaning for the person who had laid it out, although that meaning would never become obvious to anyone save the one who had put everything together. It made almost too much sense, infinitely more than the derisory amount of it that an ordinary mind resigns itself to making of the opaque and nearly mute world: and things, set apart from their usual functions, whether symbolic or practical, were reincorporated within that particular order with a different sign, in the same way as those objects of technological civilization which, after being lost in the jungle, are found by an unknown tribe and integrated into the necessary evolution of a cosmography that has existed since the night of time and that claims to have foreseen, at a precise point in the future, the ineluctable appearance of those objects.

Like the figures of certain sculptures which emerge, fragmentary yet recognizable, from the rough stone, from the chaos of overturned chairs, of broken dishes, of scattered books with pages torn out, of burns, of catsup stains, of ashes, of blood, of excrement, of torn clothing, of lamps fallen to the floor, and of armchairs eviscerated with thrusts of a knife, from which twisted springs and clumps of stuffing came tumbling out, there remained legible signs of what had happened the night before. There had been a dinner for two persons and, probably after dinner, a game of cards, since the cards were still laid out on a little table, on which there were also two miraculously untouched glasses of champagne and several colored chips that served to keep track of the score. The usual ceremony of that religion in which the officiant was at once the god and the demiurge, the doctrine and the interpretation, the church and the believer, the redemption and the punishment, the alpha and the omega in a word, had interrupted the game of cards at the very moment at which the sacrificial victim was winning, to judge from the little pile of chips lying next to her, and the fact that it was her place could be unequivocally deduced from the state of the overturned chair lying on the floor on that side of the table, and from the drops of blood staining the little pile of winning chips. As for little old lady number twenty-eight, she was lying stretched out on the same table on which the dinner had been served, to judge from the broken dishes, the remains of roast beef, baked potatoes, cheese, salad and chocolate cake adorning the floor around the table. Morvan deduced that, because of her weary bones, her frequent pains in the legs and hips, her weak heart and her lungs bloated by an early stage of emphysema, the owner of the apartment, in order not to be obliged to get up from the table every few minutes, had chosen to set all the courses to be served at one end of the table and reserve the other for eating the dinner properly so called, thereby affording her more rest and greater intimacy. To say that in life she must have had means, judging from the obviously more than comfortable air that the apartment had had before the hurricane, that she perhaps enjoyed a good retirement pension and even a nice fat income, is to waste time on superfluous details, on trivialities, given its appearance at that moment, so far removed from any idea of a social background and even of a morphologically human entity. Even before having subjected her to the work of the knife, the meticulous demiurge, after having chosen her, in all likelihood by pure chance, in one of those unpredictable encounters that opportunity creates, as the object of his ritual, had stripped her of every concrete feature, flesh, nerves, feelings, memory, granting her only the possibility of being for one night the tangible incarnation of a principle against which he was totally at war. When alive she had been rather thin, and perhaps pretty when young, and doubtless, despite her advanced age, in the dead of winter, treated herself to head-to-foot tanning sessions in a salon because, though wrinkled, her skin had the same dark cast all over, a rather pleasing color, into which the pallor of death had not managed to steal. But, and kindly excuse my insistence, it would also be necessary to agree on the word death, and if we accept that only the subject is accorded the privilege of dying, at this juncture the very notion of death disappears. The man, or whatever it was, had tied her to the table, face up, with a heavy cord across her forehead that ran underneath the table and kept her head motionless, another across her thighs and a third that immobilized her feet. He had put adhesive tape over her mouth to keep her from crying out and then, while she was probably still alive, he had opened up, with the electric knife that was still plugged in, an enormous gash that went from her throat to her pubis. Then he had turned the lips of the wound to the outside, so that the shape of the slit made it look like an enormous vagina – it was hard to say whether that had been the intention of the artist who had worked her flesh, but it was harder still to keep from immediately making such an association. Drained of blood, with its viscera removed, perhaps because of its wrinkles as well, the body seemed more like a deflated plastic doll, or better still, the dark skin of a fruit long since rotted, or, and this is perhaps the best comparison, an empty burlap bag from which a furious hand had just removed the stuffing that it contained and scattered it all over the room.

As the policeman, obeying an order from Morvan, phoned the Special Bureau from the bedroom, Morvan inspected the apartment. In one corner of the living room he found an empty champagne bottle, which must have rolled to the floor when the murderer laid his victim on the operating table. The kitchen was quite tidy, except that the silverware drawer was open and dirty serving dishes and plates were piled up in the sink where the mistress of the house had doubtless put them temporarily so as to place them in the dishwasher when the visitor had left. The refrigerator did not have very much inside it: butter, a carton of milk, eggs, four low-fat yogurts and an extra bottle of champagne. The bedroom was also in order – the policeman had already finished talking with the Special Bureau – so Morvan took only a quick look and headed to the bathroom in which, after turning the light on, he remained for a longer time. There was no definite clue, apart from the fact that the shower had been used recently, but only the laboratory would be able to determine by whom and in what circumstances, and yet in this spot Morvan had the sensation of proximity and imminence that made him so anxious. He examined the fixtures, the washbasin, the bidet, the bathtub, the medicine cabinet, the mirror, with an interest so intense that he went over the polished surface that reflected him centimeter by centimeter without noticing his own image which, since their eyes did not once meet, seemed as indifferent to him as he was to it. He was certain that it was in that room with white tiled walls that gleamed in the overly bright electric light and reflected, in a somewhat vaguer way, what was taking place in front of them, that the man, or whatever it was, that then went to the living room to torture his victims, turned into a monster, that it was probably there that he stripped naked, carefully folding his clothes so that no trace of the ceremony would remain on them, and that it was there that he returned to take a shower and get dressed, and then go out into the street, double-locking the door behind him, once again inside the human envelope that enabled him to melt into the crowd. In that parenthesis of nudity there was let loose in him what in the monotony of gray days with no way out lay drowsing, dark, densely matted, and the bathroom was the sacrosanct place where the unknown god, having chosen him for some mysterious reason from among that almost infinite multitude that so closely resembled him, became incarnate in him.

After a while, Combes came by, along with the doctor, the photographer, the men from the laboratory and the rest of the team from the bureau, but without Lautret, who was off somewhere, and Juin, who wasn't scheduled to come on duty until just past noon. Laconically, rather distantly, Morvan explained to him what he wanted and left him in charge of the rest of the operations. He would come back to his office around lunch time. On the ground floor, the concierge, in the company of a policewoman, was weeping, her head resting in the palm of her hand, her elbow on the table, clutching a paper tissue in her other hand resting in her lap. Morvan, passing by the open door, pretended not to see her and went out into the street. It was close to eight-thirty by now, but it was still dark out, the air a deep blue but already presaging the uniform gray that was about to set in until nightfall. Morvan began to walk down the Rue de la Roquette toward the Place Léon Blum. On certain stretches of the sidewalk, the layer of snow was still intact, and to Morvan it felt quite hard beneath the soles of his shoes, but he was leaving footprints in the crunchy white stuff. As there was a sort of low-lying mist, the sky properly so called was not yet visible, so that when Morvan raised his head to study it, he could not decide whether it was going to snow again or not. The food stores, greengrocers', butcher shops, bakeries, dairy stores, had already opened, but many were still empty, so that with their clerks standing motionless behind the counters, and their merchandise arranged in almost decorative displays in the windows and glass cases, the lighted shops seemed more like full-sized models of themselves than real places of business, and the glass doors shut tight because of the cold outside heightened that illusion. Morvan went into the Relais, and standing leaning on the counter, drank a café au lait in which he little by little dunked, with inordinately cautious gestures so as to keep from staining his overcoat, a croissant. A mortal anxiety had just come over him, a nameless melancholy, like a physical weariness, and so sudden and unfamiliar to him that, pushing his hat slightly back, he felt his forehead with the back of his hand to see if he had a fever. But despite the high temperature in the bar, the skin on his forehead was cold. After a few minutes, the state passed, leaving in his limbs a sort of spongy softness that he attributed to fatigue and to the events that had abruptly gotten him out of bed. Then he left the bar and walked across the square. The little decorative bulbs on the municipal

building and along the Boulevard Voltaire were still on, and
doubtless would remain on all day long, and probably all the
rest of the month, because of the dark day that was beginning.
Morvan walked slowly inside the Special Bureau, gave a
number of orders to the personnel on duty, and shut himself
up in his office.

He locked the door, took off his gloves, hat, overcoat,
draped them carefully over a chair and then, without turning
the light on, went over to the window. Sharp-pointed icicles
hung from the bare branches of the plane trees, and the
upper part of their trunks was covered with snow. Seen from
above, the sidewalks gave off bluish vibrations and the
footsteps of the first pedestrians were already beginning to
stir up the snow and create in the middle of the sidewalk a
dirty, troubled trail. The snow left intact on certain stretches
of the sidewalks and streets, and on the cornices of the facades
and the windowsills, the immaculate white masses, again
made him think of the unbearably white bull of the book of
myths of his childhood, which his father had brought him as
a gift when he came home from one of his trips, with which
he had never parted and which he still enjoyed leafing through
every once in a while; the bull with the horns in the shape of
a half-moon, which after having abducted her on a beach in
Tyre or Sidon, he no longer remembered which, feigning
gentleness at first so as to gain her trust, once he had her
seated on his muscular back, took the nymph across the sea
to Crete and raped her beneath a plane tree, thereby
occasioning the promise of the gods, unfulfilled like so many
others, that plane trees would never lose their leaves; the
white bull, he too a god, astute, at once hidden and in plain
sight, neither cruel nor magnanimous, with one half of his

being in shadow and the other in full light, with no other reason or law save his violent desire bent, in his inordinate self-affirmation, upon making rivers run backward to their source, on halting the sun in its monotonous periodic course and drawing out of their motionless state to dance and die, out of sheer caprice, in the firmament, one by one, the stars.

Morvan turned around, opened the locker, and carefully removing from it the ashtray full of bits of paper so as to keep them from flying about, sat down at his desk and turned on the lamp. He gently poured the contents of the ashtray onto the smooth surface of the desk, and unhurriedly began to spread out the little pieces of paper and assemble something like a jigsaw puzzle, selecting the bits one by one so as to fit them in with those already in place, and removing them and placing them back in the pile if they didn't fit. He thought of nothing as he did so, of nothing other than the next little piece of paper to be inserted in the corresponding empty space. It took him a good while to reconstruct the entire page of the ministerial letter, and when he had put all the bits of paper together, he was able to see that only one of them was missing, no bigger than a twenty-centime piece, in the place where the signature of the bureaucrat at the Ministry who had sent the letter in the Minister's name belonged, so that a part of the signature and of the superposed ministerial seal were needed to complete the page. Morvan removed from his pocket the little plastic envelope the size of a pack of cigarettes, pressed down on the stiff upper edges to widen the opening of it, and placing the envelope face down, began to shake it until there fell out on the desk the little piece of paper that he had collected from the bright green carpeting in the small tidy vestibule that no one, since the day before, at any event no one since the crime, had crossed through, except the man or whatever it was that, after wielding the electric knife as a sculptor wields the hammer and chisel, had gone to take a shower in the bathroom, had dressed unhurriedly, and after checking to make certain that he was leaving no trace of himself behind, had double-locked the door behind him and kept the key. The night before, he had committed his first careless misstep. After he had perhaps turned out the light in the vestibule, the little piece of paper had fallen to the floor, and as he closed the outside door, a slight draft had blown it to the center of the bright green carpeting, quite visible, white, gleaming almost, halfway between the front door and the one separating the vestibule from the inside rooms. Since the bit of paper had fallen on the desk with its white reverse side showing, Morvan slowly turned it over and saw that, in fact, on the obverse side there were several fragments of handwriting and part of a seal, so he very carefully inserted it in the empty space in the letter that had yet to be filled in, where the bit of paper fitted exactly: the puzzle was finally complete.

Morvan leaned back in his chair, and crossing his hands on his belly, sat there motionless with his eyes fixed on the ceiling. In the features of his face there was no particularly emphatic expression, nor did his body denote any particular emotion, except for the immobility of his eyes, open far too wide, his head and hands far too still, his body far too motionless in the chair, in the silence in the room suddenly far too perceptible. The image of Captain Lautret tossing the fragments of the letter in the air and the slow rain of little white bits of paper, which had scattered all over the room, also lingered in his mind, despite the slight tumult they evoked, in the utmost silence. It was evident that, at the moment it fell, the little piece of paper had adhered to or been caught on some part of the body or the clothing of one of the four police officers present, a pocket, a fold of a jacket or pair of pants, a lock of hair, the inside of a glove, a hat band, or trapped in the rough wool threads of a sweater, magnetized by static electricity, marking the man who for hours had been carrying it about on his person without knowing it, more indelibly and more unmistakably than if it had been a tattoo imprinted on his forehead with a white-hot brand, a discreet and very slight sign in the beginning which, however, in a single night had become clear evidence and had acquired the weight of a condemnation, and once white, was now the color of perdition.

After a few minutes' immobility, Morvan once again leaned over toward the reconstructed letter and contemplated it for a moment. The irregular lines formed by the jagged edges of paper where the bits, all of them of a similar size, joined together imperfectly, seemed like the tortuous threads of a spider's web, and, for a few seconds, Morvan had the extremely fleeting impression that he was the one who was trapped and lay struggling in the center of it. But that unexpected impression passed immediately, and his predilection for clarity occupied him for a good while as he went through a series of reasonings. The first thing that came to mind was that his discovery had not greatly surprised him, and that at the moment when he had seen the little piece of paper standing out against the bright green fabric, he had immediately guessed its source. To tell the truth it had been, not a discovery, but the confirmation of a certainty, a sort of tacit conviction which he had never thought of, but which had been with him day and night for months. The proximity of the shadow that he had been pursuing, Morvan knew, was not only psychological but also physical. The greyhound and its prey occupied the center of the same space, and it was from the same point that both emerged to trace the two circles that increasingly restricted their respective fields of operation. The same magic horizon hemmed them within an unbreathable space with no way out, condemning each of them to repeat, on his respective side, the same antagonistic gestures, which nonetheless were very nearly wholly complementary. In a certain sense, the greyhound was also a prey, and the prey, a greyhound. A well-nigh unbearable feeling of recognition and of identification came over Morvan, so viscerally obscene that, rather than terrifying him, made him give, as he did whenever he recognized an obvious truth, amid slow and dubious shakes of his head, a sarcastic little laugh.

Morvan distanced himself, not without reluctance, from the four men who had been exposed, as to a fatal dose of radiation, to the rain of little bits of paper, since he knew that, when the time came for proofs, all of the arguments that he was beginning to marshal against the three others, they in turn, by the same logic, could use against him. He thought he had perhaps made a mistake in keeping the only tangible proof that the murderer of the Rue de la Folie Regnault had, the evening before, as darkness was falling, come out of his office, and he could not even count on the testimony of the police officer or the concierge, because that little piece of paper, which to Morvan constituted irrefutable proof, meant nothing to them. They had seen nothing more than a bit of paper whose meaning they knew nothing of, as they knew nothing of its origin. Even a test for fingerprints would not be of much use, in the first place because in all likelihood the fingerprints of all four of them would show up on the letter, and above all because, by having kept the little piece of paper, Morvan had invalidated it as proof. There was now no means of proving that that bit of paper had ever left his office.

Although his own conduct produced in him a slight discomfort, if not a certain mild surprise, Morvan lost interest in the problem, and began to address that of the identity of the man he was pursuing. Since he had known his three collaborators for years, he found it difficult to imagine in one or another of them the great dark zone of insanity that had been necessary in order to commit that horrible series of crimes. Combes and Juin were simple-hearted men, of average intelligence, two run-of-the-mill but efficient and loyal police officers who had always worked under him and whom he had brought with him for that reason to the Special Bureau. They had no ideas of their own, but they were punctilious bureaucrats, and even though those categories seemed ridiculous to him when set alongside the crimes that had been committed, at the same time he did not believe them capable of developing the talent for dissimulation that a double life required. Moreover, both of them were married and had children. Morvan knew that that didn't mean anything, and that any responsible and affectionate family man is capable of cohabiting with a bloodthirsty monster, a fact that had been proved time and time again, but his objection was not of a moral order but a logical, and even practical, one, since he found it difficult to believe that a wife, or any other member of the family who lived under the same roof, would be unable to detect any anomaly, strangeness or peculiarity in a relative who had committed twenty-eight crimes in nine months. The least suspicious wife of the most perfect dissembler could not have helped but notice something odd on one or another of the twenty-eight times at which her husband was preparing to, or had just gone through with, torturing, raping, decapitating and quartering an old lady. From the beginning, Morvan had reasoned that the murderer lived by himself and that probably his profession, or a privileged position, allowed him to win his victims' trust. As police officers, Combes and Juin readily met the second requirement, but as heads of families, Juin in particular, who, in addition to his wife and children, had taken his mother-in-law in to live beneath the same roof, they did not satisfy the first one. The image of the solitary, faceless man, preparing to leave, in a sort of hypnotic trance, his apartment in semidarkness, incapable of turning a deaf ear to the terrible, periodic call of nightfall, did not fit the conventional picture of the family reunion at the end of the day, the children home eating their after-school snack in front of the television set, and the adults, dead tired and more or less in a daze on leaving work, preparing to have dinner. It is true that a police officer could have easily justified to his family a daily schedule that was out of the ordinary and long and frequent absences, but it was clear that the man, or whatever it was, that had committed all those crimes, had built, before beginning the series, a wall of solitude, or rather, a sort of *cordon sanitaire* around himself, a vacuum with an atmosphere all its own that no other human being could breathe without endangering his life, a desolate, sterile circle within which every living thing that, whether by mistake or deliberate calculation, had contrived to enter would immediately be transformed into a little heap of charred dust. The aura that accompanied him must have aroused feelings or emotions more highly colored, more intense – respect, envy, admiration, desires to seduce or be seduced, to obey or be obeyed, fear, hatred and even inexplicable compassion, suspicion or blind trust – than the dullness, the conventional deference and the gray professional interchanges characteristic of inspectors Combes and Juin. The animal that he was searching for was clever, excessive, calculating and cruel; he was violent and meticulous, and although he was a loner, unlike many of his contemporaries, who have no life at all, he lived more than one at the same time. In him logical thought and inexplicable acts coexisted. He lived so intoxicated by the poison that circulated all through his being, in his blood perhaps, from the very instant that he emerged into the air of this world, that he was unaware of, or indifferent to, his own cruelty. He might have casual and even long-standing friends, but when two friends part it is truly difficult for each of them to know what the other has done during the hours, the days, the weeks or the months of separation. It is already hard to have any idea of what he may be doing when he goes downstairs for ten minutes, on the pretext of buying cigarettes at the bar on the corner, or even during the seconds when we cease to have him in our visual field when we turn around to take a book down from the library shelf. Probably he moved frequently, or perhaps he had more than one apartment, a fixed domicile and another that he used off and on, for professional reasons, like the little bedrooms in the Special Bureau for example, which the four police officers occupied when they were on duty or when, as might well be the case with Morvan, they got off work late and didn't feel like leaving. The man, or whatever it was, also possessed great physical strength, since otherwise he would not have been able to handle the corpses as he did when he took it into his head to slit them open or hack them to pieces, and he was also cautious and careful, as proved by the fact that, of the first twenty-seven crimes, he had not left a single sign that might incriminate him. That detail might also prove that he was a police officer, because he was intelligent enough to eliminate every compromising trace, knowing beforehand what his colleagues would be searching for. And as for those signs he did leave, a hair (if it was really his), sperm, some other trifle, he was perfectly aware that they could be of value as a clue on a comparative basis, but that no single one constituted, in and of itself, proof. The sperm, however, Morvan thought he left deliberately, because he enjoyed letting it be known that there had been a rape. Morvan had known for a long time that he dressed well and was fairly good-looking, perhaps above average, since several old ladies had allowed themselves to be tempted by his charms before the ritual properly speaking. That, of course, was not enough in this day and age: he also had to inspire trust, and in order to gain it his police credentials must have been very useful to him. Perhaps he approached them on the street, or telephoned them to tell them that he would be coming by to see if everything was going well and if the orders concerning public safety were being carried out properly, and in many instances he may have given them the phone number of the Special Bureau so that they could call him, which must have increased their trust. Perhaps he saw some of them several times before getting himself invited to dinner, or perhaps he arrived on purpose just at the aperitif or dinner hour, and relieving the old lady's loneliness with his entertaining and protective conversation, he had no difficulty in getting himself invited to stay on for dinner. He may even have phoned from the bureau, announcing his visit, and arriving with a bottle, a box of bonbons, a book or a videocassette as a gift. His police credentials were perhaps not always sufficient to reassure the mistress of the house and gain her trust. It could be that the man or whatever it was, for some precise reason, had a more familiar face then his other colleagues. Morvan was already well-known in the whole neighborhood because of his regular patrols and his long diurnal strolls and above all his nocturnal ones, as well as the fact that he too had visited many buildings more than a few times to inspect them and that he had been in many private apartments and concierges' lodges to see if the orders concerning public safety that had been widely broadcast were really being applied, but despite his constant presence in the field of operations, his person was relatively less well-known than that of other colleagues, Captain Lautret for example, who appeared several times a week on television and personally addressed his orders, face to face one might say, to the terrified old ladies, from the tube, as they say. It was obvious that, of all the Crime Squad, Lautret was the best-known member, thanks to television, which had made of him, after nine months of weekly communiqués, a quite popular figure. Lautret would not even have had to use his credentials to enter, not only old ladies' apartments, but whatever place he was of a mind to, and not only in the neighborhood where the crimes were committed, but in the entire city and even the whole country. The repulsive shadow that came out, every so often, impelled by an urgent need, whose iron laws he blindly, repeatedly obeyed, in order to strike, perhaps took, so as to hide himself, and in view of everyone, the colored, protective and familiar form of a television image, so that he had already made himself quite at home, long before knocking on the door, in the intimacy and the credulity of his victims. Without emotion and without being surprised at that absence of emotion, Morvan realized what the anxious sensation of proximity that he had had for some time – and that a little later would grow to the point of turning into dementia – had caused him to have a presentiment of, namely, that his old friend Captain Lautret was the man that he was looking for.

"I would have bet my head on it," Tomatis says.

"Tomatis!" Pigeon exclaims, calling him by his surname with the aim of parodying a reproachful tone of voice. And then: "We're not in a gambling den."

"In any case, he has a mortgage hanging over his head," Soldi says. "He couldn't bet it even if he wanted to."

Tomatis raises his hands to his chest, the palms, of a lighter color than the tanned backs, facing outward, so as to defend himself from attacks, criticisms and objections, and shaking the head that according to Soldi has a supposed mortgage hanging over it, proffers with an apodictic and professorial air:

"I mean to say that the solution seemed obvious to me from the start."

"The truth is," Pigeon says, "that at this point in the story we've arrived, not at the solution, but at the beginning of the problem."

"Cheap suspense," Tomatis says, addressing not Pigeon but Soldi, yet gesturing to Pigeon with a meaningful nod of his head which, translated into words, might be read as: *I call your attention to the scarcely recommendable methods that this individual is using to pull the wool over our eyes with his story.*

"We'll soon see," Pigeon says. "For now let's have something to eat."

The words he has just uttered have coincided with the arrival of the waiter, whom he has seen coming toward the table along the powdered brick path. The first three glasses have been empty for some time now, so that, aware that he has made them wait, the waiter begins to deposit on the table three other blond beers, topped with a generous head of white foam, setting down immediately thereafter various dishes, namely salami already peeled and cut into slices, a little pot of green olives in oil, a couple of portions of pizza à la napolitana (tomato, mozzarella and oregano) that, no doubt cut out of an entire circle of pizza, must have had for a few instants a triangular shape, but are now being put before them divided into many subportions of irregular geometrical form, and lastly, after the little metal basket full of oval slices of bread, the main dish, that is to say veal scallops à la milanese, still warm, garnished with pickles and juicy yellow quarters of lemon. Toothpicks, silverware, salt, Savora, plus the *de rigueur* appetizers that accompany beer, complete the unloading of the tray on which, once there is nothing left on it, the waiter begins to load the glasses and the little empty plates of appetizers.

"I trust we won't have to wait so long for the next ones," Tomatis says, in a mock pleading tone of voice that, at bottom, is a warning or a reproach.

"No," the waiter says. "It was because they were changing over to a new keg."

"I would have bet as much. I could tell by the look of the head on it," Tomatis says.

The waiter pretends not to hear and only Tomatis laughs at his own rejoinder, which has supposedly been witty and not intended to be hurtful, but which has given the impression of offending the waiter, who, making no comment, goes off toward the bar. Pigeon waits till he is far enough away from the table to upbraid Tomatis.

"I'd forgotten your incorruptible purism."

"Etherythig thould be a perfecht thpecimen of its kaing," Tomatis says, his mastication of an irregular trapezoid of hot pizza making pronunciation difficult, obliging him to modify his sibilants and transforming the *d* of the word "kind" into a drawn-out nasal. Pigeon turns toward Soldi.

"I grant that he adheres to his own credo," he says.

Raising a bit of bread to his mouth, Soldi silently nods and then, as he chews, fixes his eyes, beyond the little white wall of balustrades and the dark street, on the low, flat-roofed bus terminal which, as he has noted several times, even though it was built twenty years before, Pigeon still calls the new terminal, for the sole reason that it was opened after his departure. More than ever, as he hears Pigeon and Tomatis talking back and forth, he has the impression that he is watching a comedy with himself as the only spectator, and wonders again whether, when they are alone together, the two friends speak of the same things in the same way. They seem so much at home in the present, so much the masters of their words and acts, so perfectly cast as different and complementary characters that they are like those actors in the middle of a performance who, for the the duration of it, enjoy the privilege of living for the outside world, or of being merely what they themselves are on the outside, safe from the raveled threads of thought, of contradictory feelings, of odd sensations and of fragmentary, incomprehensible and voracious images, independent of all logic and of all will, which form the intimate texture of life. They give the impression of being protected from their inner sensations, from indecision, from anxiety. For a few seconds, Soldi judges them harshly, but almost immediately, and unexpectedly, he asks himself if they are not really like that, merely exterior, and so in accord with themselves, and so resigned to the monotonous, dangerous flow, with no meaning and no solution, of life that, by dint of no longer hoping for anything from it, they have acquired a sort of serenity.

It is evident that he is mistaken. For example, of the day just past, each one of them is bringing away, not only shared experiences, images, sensations, memories of his own that are inaccessible to language and incommunicable, so to speak, till the end of eternity, but also the irritation of old wounds that both of them believe to have healed over and that, to a very slight degree naturally, have begun to bleed again. At the time of Cat's and Elisa's disappearance, Héctor and Tomatis took it upon themselves to do everything necessary to try to locate them, with no results moreover, but Pigeon refused to come, arguing that in any event they would not reappear and that he now had another family in Europe that was depending on him, and on which he depended, and that he was not prepared to part from it. Héctor kept him regularly informed of their searches until finally, not obtaining any result, they abandoned them, but for nearly two years, Tomatis and Pigeon stopped writing to each other. To tell the truth, Tomatis stopped answering Pigeon's letters, and it took the latter several months to understand the reason for the silence and forbear to go on writing to him. And then, after two years had gone by, when Pigeon least expected it, it was Tomatis who began the correspondence again with an inordinately long letter, in which he told him that, after months and months of bitter and contradictory reflections, he had finally realized that the excessive prudence on Pigeon's part was really fear, though not fear of meeting, as people say, the same fate as his brother, but, on the contrary, fear of confronting direct proof that that inconceivable duplicate being, so different from many points of view, and yet so intimately linked to him beginning in the very womb of their mother that it was impossible for him to perceive and to conceive of the universe in any other way than through sensations and thoughts that seemed to stem from the same senses and the same intelligence, could have disappeared without a trace in the air of this world, or worse still, that in his stead he might be presented with a little anonymous pile of bones removed from an unknown plot of earth.

That afternoon, on the return from Washington's, when from the launch he showed his son the house in Rincón at the bend of the Ubajay, it seemed to Pigeon that Tomatis's expression darkened slightly. Despite the calm movement of the launch, the benevolent breeze blowing, the afternoon sun that lessened the fever of the hot day a little, Pigeon has a bitter memory of that moment, and not only because of Tomatis, but also because of his own son, the deliberate apathy of whose reaction did not altogether succeed in hiding a violent emotion, which Pigeon attributes to the painful images that the adolescent still retains of the terrible days following the disappearance of Cat and Elisa. His two sons had seen him cry for the first time, and wander about the house with reddened eyes, insensible to anything exterior to himself, for weeks on end. So that Soldi is mistaken if he believes that Pigeon and Tomatis, monolithic and apparently at their ease in the present, are immune to the constant tug of war or the crackle that, as in the starry sky, explodes at every moment within the inner darkness. What happens is that, through a sort of stylistic complicity, acquired after years of acquaintance, crystallized in a tacit convention, they have learned not to show it too openly.

Moreover, the sensation of being in the presence of a slightly different Pigeon disturbs Tomatis. When he has seen him lean over the dactylogram, in Washington's work room, it has seemed to him that he was manifesting a feigned, condescending interest, and because of this, Tomatis has felt a slight humiliation, thinking that perhaps local conflicts leave Pigeon indifferent, and a little later the thought has crossed his mind that it has been more out of courtesy than out of genuine interest that, on the boat trip back, Pigeon has asked Soldi for an oral summary of the novel. Although he has maintained with him, with regard to the dactylogram, a frequent and lively correspondence, Tomatis is of the opinion that, as happens with so many other things, places, objects, loves, as the imaginary anticipation of the experience is always more intense than the experience itself, on arriving in the city Pigeon has been suddenly overtaken by indifference, boredom or lack of zest. In any event, Pigeon's evident apathy, that in Cat went so far as impassibility and at times apparent cruelty, which the liveliness of his letters has made him forget, on occasion has for Tomatis, and Tomatis does not forbear to keep it in the clear zone of his mind so as to analyze it coldly, something unacceptable and hurtful about it.

But all this does not have the least influence on their relations. Each of them blames the situation on himself, and just as Tomatis thinks that the cause of that sense of humiliation must be sought within himself and not in Pigeon's demeanor, Pigeon has been secretly reproaching himself for several years now for not having come at the time of Cat's and Elisa's disappearance and ever since he has come back to the city, he has been of the opinion that his not having liked or even visited the house in Rincón and his mother's apartment before the sale is a prolongation of this attitude. In his heart of hearts, he permits and accepts the interpretation that others may have of his behavior, and those others are actually two individuals, Héctor and Tomatis. But for the moment Héctor is in Europe – Pigeon has frequently put him up in Paris in recent years – so that Tomatis is his only judge, and even though he knows that Tomatis will never express it in words, looks or meaningful reactions, Pigeon has decided, whatever it may be, to regard his verdict, before the fact, as being a fair one.

"What I mean to say," Tomatis says, leaning over the platter of veal scallops with determination, and resuming the conversation interrupted by the arrival of the waiter, "is that the greyhound and his prey, to use your own words, always reason in the same way."

"We agree there," Pigeon says. "But I want to tell you the story to the very end. It came out in all the papers."

"Is that supposed to prove that it's true?" Soldi objects, opening his mouth hidden by his black beard, like a cave by a tangle of charred vegetation, and popping into his open mouth a dark green olive, and almost immediately thereafter, without even having spat out the pit, a reddish slice of salami. And as he chews, he thinks that that argument, so often brandished by Tomatis, must have seemed to Pigeon like a proof of the excessive, and perhaps corrupting, influence that Tomatis exercises over his person. He is almost ashamed of having put it forward, but his instinct of preservation leads him to think that, after all, he is young, intelligent, rich, cultivated, and that he has his whole life ahead of him, so that it is of little importance that the genuine affection he feels for Tomatis can be interpreted by others as a sign of servility.

"I'm not talking about the veracity of the story, but about my own," Pigeon says. "If you don't believe me, I'll send you the papers."

Vacillating, Soldi spits the olive pit in the palm of his hand, and then deposits it in an ashtray. Tomatis notes his hesitation.

"Don't pay any attention to him," he says. "It's a commonplace of French criticism."

Pigeon bursts out laughing.

"No, really," he says. "It came out in all the papers. And what's more, it happened around the corner from my house."

"An irrefutable argument," Soldi says disdainfully, recovering his aplomb and again adopting the tone being employed in the conversation, consisting, in the last analysis, of formulating, ironically, objections or approbations, without ever being quite certain that they have been accepted or even understood by the others. "Unfortunately, the author of *In the Greek Tents* has already addressed this problem."

In a somewhat ostentatious and conventional manner,

Pigeon raises his eyebrows and assumes an interrogative expression, intended to mean more or less: *from the information concerning this text that you have communicated to me, I would not have gathered the impression that it dealt with this question.*

"The two soldiers," Soldi says. "The two soldiers on guard in Menelaus's tent."

And in view of the interest shown by Pigeon and Tomatis, which to a slight degree stimulates and intoxicates him, and which is quite apparent – perhaps a little too much so – from their expressions, Soldi explains that of the Old Soldier and the Young Soldier – the two main characters of the novel – the Young Soldier, who has arrived from Sparta only a few days before, is the one who knows the most about the war. The Old Soldier, who has been on the plain of Scamander for ten years – the majority of the novel takes place on the night preceding the introduction of the Horse into the city and hence its destruction – has not once seen a Trojan, at any rate not from up close, owing perhaps to the fact that he is a member of Menelaus's staff, which takes care of the problems of supply and security in the rear guard, and to him the word *Trojan* calls to mind only a few tiny human figures, fighting against the Greeks at one point on the plain, and then at another, and later on at another, and so on. When Menelaus, at the beginning of the siege, heading an embassy, had entered the city to reclaim Helen (whom he had never seen), it had been his turn to stand guard out in the camp. And if a Trojan embassy came to parley, it was always in Agamemnon's tent that it was received. For him, therefore, Troy was a gray wall in the distance on which, from time to time, he saw a vaguely human silhouette walking about. Of the exploits of the hero whose sleep they were watching over at that very moment, the Old Soldier knew almost nothing, perhaps because in all the years that he had been in his service, his chief had spoken to him only two or three times. The Young Soldier, on the other hand, was familiar with all the events, down to the most insignificant of them, that had taken place since the beginning of the siege. And not only he, but all Greece, which was tantamount to saying the entire universe. All the facts relating to the war were familiar even to the most obscure Greek. Even the children who had been born four or five years after the beginning of the hostilities, imitated the most salient events in their games: they all wanted to be Achilles, Agamemnon, Ulysses, and only against their will did they accept the role of Paris, of Hector, of Antenor. Even the ones who were still crawling about on all fours wanted to go recover Patroclus's dead body, just as full-grown men, standing straight and tall on vigorous limbs, adopted in the public square attitudes that they believed imitated Philoctetes or Ajax, or as oldsters who, helping themselves along with a cane, which they would often twirl in the fever of their stories, went up and down the roads repeating the feats that everyone knew by heart and yet never tired of hearing about. On winter nights, when snow fell in the lonely mountains, whole families, masters and servants, lords and slaves, men and women, adults and children, huddled round the fire to listen, for the thousandth time, to the stories. If a traveler, making his way along in some deserted spot met a stranger or a shepherd who had been tending his flock for months in some remote valley, once they had exchanged a conventional greeting the subject of the war came up in the conversation. On his return from one of these summer pastures, a certain shepherd maintained that one morning his goats, inexplicably, had begun to bleat disconsolately, and that he had learned shortly thereafter from a traveler that this had occurred on the day of Patroclus's death. In the Old Soldier's head, all these names of heroes were mixed up, because he had very little contact with them and was unaware of most of the deeds that seemed so glorious to the Young Soldier. To the Old Soldier the few tangible effects of the war were summed up in two or three concrete facts: one day, for example, after a battle that everyone said had been very violent, but that he had seen nothing of save for a cloud of dust at a distant point on the plain, his chief had returned slightly wounded, and on several other occasions as well he had been able to deduce, from Menelaus's mood, whether the course of events was favorable or unfavorable to the Greeks. One thing seemed certain: there was a war going on, because some of his old comrades who had been sent into action never came back to camp, and because sometimes bread and oil were in short supply – never at the leader's table naturally – and other such things, the whole of them being a sign of hard times. If he had run across Ulysses or Agamemnon, the Old Soldier would not have recognized them. When the other leaders came to Menelaus's tent, they always did so in a group, and when they came alone, it was equally hard for the Old Soldier to distinguish them. In any event, at his age – in reality he was barely forty years old – he had already learned some time before that it is best for a mere foot soldier to be blind, deaf and dumb and try to pass altogether unnoticed. For the Young Soldier it was precisely the opposite: he had never seen Helen either, but he knew all the stories, anecdotes and legends about her that were making the rounds. He probably knew more about her than her husband and the Trojan lover – to the Old Soldier the name Paris meant nothing – who, violating the laws of hospitality, had seduced and abducted her in Menelaus's absence. What was more: he maintained that Helen was the most beautiful woman in the world, and he also regarded her as the most chaste, because a king of Egypt who had lodged the couple during a halt on their journey to Troy, on learning of the abduction, banished Paris and, thanks to magical manipulations, fashioned a simulacrum of Helen so closely resembling the original that Paris had taken her to Troy with him believing that she was the real one, who, according to what the Young Soldier had heard, was still in Egypt, where she had aged considerably, awaiting her husband's return. To which the Old Soldier answered (memorably according to Soldi, and in the novel with better chosen words than the ones that he was passing on to them in an abridged version) that, if all that was true, the cause of that war was a simulacrum, which in a certain sense changed nothing insofar as he was concerned, because in view of the little he knew about it, not only the cause of it, but also the war itself was a simulacrum and that, if he were some day to return to Sparta and someone asked him to tell about the war, he would find himself in a delicate situation, but if a little leisure fell to his lot in his old age, he would devote it to learning more about all those events that were so well-known throughout the world and that the Young Soldier had just related to him.

Pleased with Soldi's long explanation, Tomatis turns his eyes away from him and studies Pigeon's face with a certain expectancy, to see whether Soldi's words have produced the effect that he would like, namely to cause Pigeon to be as interested in the novel as in the personality of the executor – appointed by the daughter thanks to the maneuvers of Tomatis himself – of Washington's literary estate. And since he is of the opinion that his own reputation depends somewhat on that effect, Pigeon's thoughtful smile reassures him. He is altogether familiar, after more than thirty-five years, with that smile, in which there is at one and the same time complicity, fellow feeling and reflection, and which always presages a rejoinder, preceded by a brief silence. And the rejoinder is forthcoming.

"The Old Soldier possesses the truth of experience and the Young Soldier the truth of fiction. They are never identical but, despite their being of a different order, at times they may not be contradictory," Pigeon says.

"That is so," Soldi says. "But the first lays claim to being more true than the second."

Pigeon leans over to stab a little piece of veal scallop with his toothpick and, lifting it as he straightens up again, holds it aloft, suspended midway in its journey to his mouth.

"I don't deny it," he says. "But why is the second so gratified at being peddled in brothels?"

"What lofty ideas!" Tomatis says with exaggerated irony, but truly pleased by the dialogue that he has just heard, though also a little out of sorts because he would have liked to join in with an intelligent observation, and despite a great deal of hard thinking none has occurred to him. So that, after downing a swallow of beer, he decides to sound Pigeon out in order to assure himself of his genuine interest in the dactylogram. This afternoon, when they were in Washington's work room, hasn't Pigeon, as he studied the dactylogram, thought certain things that he has preferred not to express aloud or was he, Tomatis, perhaps mistaken? And on hearing him, Pigeon bursts out laughing, like the practical joker who has just been discovered as he is readying himself to spring his joke, and with that laugh he not only underscores the innocent nature of his maneuvers, but also the perspicacity of the one who has discovered them. Pigeon says that, in fact, the first thing he realized, on fixing his eyes on the copy of *In the Greek Tents,* was the fact that Washington could not possibly have been the author, but that his instinct of self-preservation had dissuaded him from offering that opinion in the presence of the daughter. Tomatis decidedly approves of Pigeon's words, with vigorous shakes of his head and repeated stabs with his toothpick at a green olive that he does not manage to land until he decides to use his fingers, but Soldi, without entirely disagreeing with Pigeon's attitude, thinks that he ought to comport himself with circumspection so as not to betray so openly the trust that Julia has placed in him. Julia's irrationality, that so vastly irritates Tomatis, arouses in him a certain compassion, and in her belated devotion to Washington's memory, it seems to him that he senses less hypocrisy or self-interest than the search, after having lost almost everything in life, for a reason that would give the end of it a meaning.

"There's no particular reason why it should be a local author," Tomatis says.

"If it's a local author, perhaps there are other copies extant in the city," Pigeon says.

"I've been making inquiries," Soldi says. "Not a trace of other copies."

"There's no particular reason why it should be a local

author," Tomatis repeats, since, at times, if he does not receive the explicit approval of his conversational partners, he is convinced, thereby putting himself at somewhat of a remove from reality, that he has not been heard. "Perhaps one of Washington's anarchist friends wrote it, during the time when he was in Buenos Aires or Paraguay, and sent him a copy in the 30s or 40s."

A sudden commotion interrupts him. Pigeon raises his head and points upward with his finger, toward the lights and the tops of the trees.

"The ballerinas," he says. "A storm."

Soldi and Tomatis raise their heads in turn: come from who knows where, from the darkness, from nothingness, thousands and thousands of white butterflies are milling about around the lights hanging from the trees and from the white walls that enclose the patio. Whirling swiftly round and round, bumping into each other, hurling themselves against the glowing garlands of lights, they produce a multiple stridence and an unexpected whitish agitation overhead, attracting the attention of the customers of the restaurant, who watch them and point them out, and introduce them, with the same sudden unpredictability with which they appeared in the patio, into the bright area of their consciences and into their conversations. The same unearthly effervescence bubbling up in the patio, Tomatis imagines, must be producing the same stir around all the lights of the city, and probably of the whole region, the same winged larvae, quivering and blind, reproduced out of sheer caprice, with dizzying simultaneity, in millions and millions of copies, having suddenly emerged from the nocturnal swamps, to shiver for a moment close to the light, and then spin feverishly downward to the dark earth, lying at last completely motionless. Tomorrow they will be like a tarpaulin of little dry flowers, fragile and fallen apart, giving not the slightest sign now of having been living matter once, a vibratory vegetable substance, a repetitive and maniacal form, scrupulously identical to itself, in which everything has been foreseen save for the ultimate end, and having come forth, like so many others, from the one abundant flow which, beneath the deceptive appearance of eternity, is no less meaningless and ephemeral.

"Yes," Tomatis says. "The ballerinas. You can bet that summer will see the end of them."

And, leaning against the back of his chair, he lets his head fall backward, endeavoring to auscultate, apparently to no result, beyond the enormous tops of the acacias and the plumes of the palms, the dark sky. Drops of sweat that have broken out on his forehead run swiftly down his temples to his ears, and when they reach the edge of his jaw, near his earlobes, they fall into space, wetting the collar of his blue shirt. The tanned skin of his face, of his arms, of his neck, seems as thick as leather, and strong, nearly impenetrable, and like leather as well, in certain portions of its surface, on his forehead, around his eyes and mouth, it is a bit withered and wrinkled. Observing him, Pigeon rejoices within himself at finding him looking so healthy, an illusion that is accentuated because Tomatis, approaching fifty, still has quite a lot of dark tousled hair. A fleeting, lightning-quick yet very intense impression of continuity or perhaps of permanence transports him as he observes him, as if the physical invariability displayed by Tomatis, who, when he was twenty seemed older than he was and now that he is almost fifty, younger than he is, constituted a proof not so much of the gentleness of time as of its nonexistence. Only the present seems real to him, and so inseparable from the density of things, so commingled with the palpable extension of the world, that its temporal dimension is as if abolished. Time and its threats now present themselves to him in the guise of a legend, at once highly colored and terrible, to which, having taken refuge in the clear, coarse roughness of the present, he no longer considers it necessary to go on lending any credence. Soldi's bright green, almost fluorescent, shirt vibrates in the night air of the patio and the sound of the ballerinas overhead, around the lights, following their sudden appearance, plus the customers seated in their white wrought iron chairs, plus the taste of the swallow of beer that he has just downed, plus the sensation of coolness which, after he has set the empty glass down on the table, has lingered on his fingertips, plus the moving background of the restaurant, with the white wall, the straw roof and the staff bustling about the bar and the kitchen and then scattering down the paths of powdered red brick, plus the motionless tops of the trees, the garlands of little colored light bulbs, the dishes and glasses on the table, all those presences at once familiar and enigmatic, as though they had just blossomed forth, clear and compact, from a lump of nothingness, seem to have blocked the flow of change, leaving it in an improbable, distant exterior, as though the raw present were unfolding in a glass ball on which drops of time, unable to adhere to the smooth transparent capsule, were sliding off toward an abyss of black, dismantled eternity.

For a few minutes, they go on eating in silence, pecking without order or method, almost as though they were mechanically obeying successive muscular tics, at the little bits of food, circular red slices of salami, dark green olives, ovoid and shiny, lying on top of a stratum of oil, irregular triangular segments of the subportions of pizza covered with an ivorine layer of melted mozzarella from beneath which there emerge little bright red patches of tomato, white flakes of popcorn, whose form, in large part aleatory, which perhaps only chaos theory could analyze, is the result of the explosion of the grains of white popcorn when the skillet reaches a certain temperature.

"There is an important detail that I have omitted up until now," Pigeon says all of a sudden, his eyes meeting, fleetingly and successively, those of his two conversational partners in order to assure himself that they are prepared to go on paying attention to him. "After the separation, Lautret began to have an intimate relationship with Caroline, Morvan's wife. Morvan, though the fact seemed obvious and, moreover, a matter of indifference to him, was suspicious of it. He did not know exactly what sort of relationship it was, but he knew that Lautret and his ex-wife saw each other frequently and that neither of the two had spoken frankly to him of these meetings. Since he had been the one who had sought the separation from Caroline, Morvan knew that he had no claim to her. He would have preferred that they act in a less secret way, though he realized that Caroline must have been the one who insisted on such discretion: despite having calmly and reasonably agreed to the separation, since they had ceased to understand each other on many planes at once, Caroline would have preferred to go on with her life in common with Morvan, whom she respected and whom she had genuinely loved for many years. In a certain sense, while it was true that she had a liaison with Lautret, it was essentially a sort of prolongation of her relations with Morvan. We must not forget that Lautret was Morvan's best friend, and that in the happiest periods of their existence, the three of them had seen each other frequently and had constituted a sort of family. To Caroline – Morvan was certain – a relationship with Lautret on the sexual plane, aside from its being an attempt to remain in the habitual circle of her affective life, was also, in a paradoxical and even contradictory way, a means of escaping from that circle with what she had closest at hand.

Lautret's case was different. Of his immature and kaleidoscopic affective life, there had remained the trace from the distant past of a couple of divorces and many conjugal storms. At certain periods, when he went to visit the Morvans, he came with a different woman every month. From his tour of duty on the Vice Squad he had maintained certain contacts in the milieu of high-class prostitutes and, although there were those who had accused him, in lowered voices, of proxenetism, Morvan knew that it was not true and that Lautret used those women within the framework of his job as a police officer, though occasionally he allowed himself to be overcome, as they say, by temptation. Lautret had acknowledged the facts in Morvan's presence, maintaining that going to bed with one of those women from time to time formed part of his professional duties. Morvan had always been convinced that, despite his methods and his lifestyle, which it goes without saying he would never have wanted for himself, Lautret was a quite honest and undoubtedly efficient police officer. Only his relationship with Caroline had, for some time now, given rise in him to a certain malaise, because it seemed to him that he sensed that Lautret, perhaps because he had idealized him to too great a degree, was attempting to replace him both on the affective plane and on the professional plane. In a certain sense, the uneasiness to which that attempt gave rise in Morvan was owed, not to the fact that he felt betrayed or threatened, but to the fact that it revealed in Lautret a certain inconsistency that made him different and vulnerable. It was as if Lautret were somewhat dependent on him and as if, despite their differences of temperament, so immediately perceptible from the outside, he were trying to identify himself, by every means possible, and with no apparent forethought, with Morvan's personality. In all likelihood, Caroline would have sensed it too, a long time before: if she had always sided with Lautret, it was not because she considered him innocent, but rather, not altogether in control of his acts. I don't know if you realize what I am trying to say."

"I think that . . ." Tomatis says.

"Shhh!" Pigeon accompanies his exaggerated hushing with a no less imperative movement of his hand, consisting of raising it and turning the palm toward Tomatis, as though he were a traffic cop ordering a truck approaching an intersection at full throttle to stop. "Your turn will come. But silence for now: I'm the one who counts here."

The waiter — as he speaks, Pigeon has seen him coming — arrives with three beers that he sets down on the table without a word, one in front of each one of the diners, and then, removing the three empty glasses from the round before, he goes off again in the direction of the bar along the reddish path of powdered brick that creaks beneath the soles of his shoes.

"You've offended him forever," Soldi says.

"That may well be," Tomatis says. "But thanks to me, the head at least is as tall now as it ought to be. And it's nice and cold."

"You aren't going to recite your draconian code to us again," Pigeon says.

"Without false modesty," Tomatis says, "I believe that this world is crying out for me to try to better it."

"In my opinion, it got worse when you came along," Pigeon says.

They're beginning their act again, is the thought that comes to Soldi, whom, when all is said and done, heaven only knows why, the story that Pigeon is telling, after having laid aside the problem of whether it is true or fictitious, has begun to interest, and the interruptions by Tomatis, who insists on constantly offering his opinion, to irritate slightly. But he is forced to recognize that Tomatis, or in any event so the expression on his face seems to indicate, is listening to Pigeon's story with profound interest, to the point, even, that at times his concentration is so great that for a few seconds he sits there with his mouth hanging open, ceasing altogether to chew. When Pigeon notices this, a faint, pleased smile crosses his lips.

"There will soon come time for you to have your say," Pigeon says, employing an enigmatic turn of phrase.

A ballerina, falling from overhead, knocks against his shoulder, slides down the yellow cloth of his shirt and, still fluttering so fast that its little white wings seem multiple and transparent, disappears into the bottom of his pocket. With the thumb and index finger of his left hand, Pigeon pulls the edge of the pocket open and looks inside, laughing. Then he puts two fingers of his right hand in it, pokes about a bit and removes the butterfly, which goes on fluttering, rapidly and excitedly, holds it for a moment in the palm of his hand, and then drops it on the ground. On his fingertips there remain traces of a fine powder, sticky and vaguely iridescent.

"That complication represented a problem for Morvan," he finally says. "Not only did it lead him to mistrust his own powers of reason, which might have been clouded by that not at all clear situation, but also, since there must have been certain of his colleagues who were aware of it, to entertain the suspicion that partiality and the lack of proof might invalidate his accusations. Morvan had realized that, if his hypothesis was correct, he was unable to share it in secret with anyone before having succeeded in proving it. He had to work alone. With his gaze fixed on the reassembled letter on top of the desk, he reflected on the odd calm with which he considered the terrible evidence that he was analyzing: his best friend, to whom for years now he had been bound by ties of affection, respect and trust, was the wild animal, the inhuman and destructive shadow that he had been chasing for nine months, and that sudden revelation had not produced within him the slightest vibration, apart from a certain faint and somewhat disdainful pride, as though he had solved a problem in logic in the face of which many others before him had failed. The solution to the problem had immediately freed him of the anxious impression of proximity, and even of familiarity, that the acts of the man, or whatever it was, had constantly given him in recent days. And it was to his lack of emotions, aside perhaps from an inexplicable, mute pity that he attributed the fact that perhaps it was not Lautret who was the author of those crimes, but a completely overlooked, parasitical force, unknown even to Lautret himself, and lodged in the intimate recesses of his being since the origins of his existence, an obscure presence resembling an archaic and bloodthirsty idol, the discovery of which would bring his friend calm and emancipation. Abruptly, the telephone buzzer began to ring, and the little bits of paper of the reassembled letter shook a little, perhaps because of the sound waves, of the inner vibrations of the apparatus that were transmitted to the desk, or of Morvan's sudden start, which in all truth was more mental than physical. The policeman on guard duty announced a call from a certain Madame Mouton, who wished to speak to Captain Lautret, but since the captain was not in the Special Bureau that morning, the woman had asked to be connected with Morvan. Intrigued, Morvan waited for a few seconds, until the still-firm voice of an elderly lady began to resound in his ear through the receiver, one of those unknown voices that come through on the phone and because of their inflections lead us almost immediately to attribute to the speaker an imaginary physiognomy. Morvan saw a woman long past maturity, still meticulous about her person, living alone in a rather comfortable apartment, and enjoying a substantial retirement pension and a fat independent income, as they say, in other words with too great an economic autonomy to resign herself to depending on anyone, even the police, but at the same time too old for her insistence, insufficiently concealed beneath a worldly tone of voice, not to allow a fair amount of anxiety to show through, and to all that Morvan added as a corollary the hypothesis that the police protection she was asking for perhaps concealed specters of some other sort. From the flood of words, Morvan managed to make out the following: she had made the acquaintance of Captain Lautret when she had once come to the Special Bureau to learn more about the alarming situation created, for elderly persons, by all those frightful crimes that were the talk of the neighborhood. The captain had been most kind to her and had promised to come visit her some night after he got off duty to see if the building in which she lived, and her apartment as well, met the safety standards that the police had recommended. The evening before she had met him by chance coming out of the supermarket, and the captain had promised her that he would come to see her the next day at eight p.m. – *today, that is,* Madame Mouton had repeated in an increasingly peremptory fashion – and she was therefore calling to remind him of the appointment. Captain Lautret had told her that his visit would be purely a routine one, simply a pretext to have an aperitif with her and strengthen the ties between the police and the neighborhood, but she had just heard on the radio the news about the crime on the Rue de la Folie Regnault, which was close to her apartment, and to tell the truth she was rather worried. If she had dared disturb Morvan, it was because Captain Lautret had also given her his name in case she needed urgent help and he, Lautret, were absent at the time. Morvan tried to reassure her and, after noting down her address and her telephone number, promised to pass the message on to Lautret. Then he hung up.

An unexpected fury clouded his mind for a moment, as though the spectacle and the consequences of twenty-eight horrible crimes had seemed less serious to him than the patient and cynical premeditation with which Lautret wove his fatal net. It seemed to him that he was able to follow, by a sort of mimetic projection, each one of the steps that Lautret's intelligence, as hard, cold and cutting as a sheet of steel, was taking in order to put together, piece by piece, the trap that he was laying. He was able to understand and even to accept the sudden violence of criminal impulses, but the obscene algebra of what was being planned had made him lose his composure for several minutes. Impatiently, he rose to his feet, clumsily moving his chair aside, and walked over to the window: despite the promise of the gods that they would never lose their leaves, because beneath one of them, in Crete, after having abducted her on a beach in Tyre or Sidon, the unbearably white bull, with horns in the shape of a half-moon, raped the terrified nymph, the plane trees along the boulevard raised their shining branches aloft, loaded with snow and sharp-pointed stalactites, cutting into irregular fragments the dark air of the December morning. For a good while, Morvan remained standing near the window, motionless, his eyes riveted on the snow stirred up and dirtied because of the footprints that the first morning pedestrians had left on the sidewalk opposite, between two intact strips of immaculate snow. The grayish, foggy half-shadow was no doubt the maximum clarity that the winter day would attain, and several hours later, shortly after lunch, darkness would again begin to close in upon him, Morvan, and upon that place called Paris, clinging for no apparent reason to that point of the earth's crust, like a rough-shelled mollusk to a no less rough, hard and fortuitous fold in a vaguely spherical rock. For a few seconds he had the odd, fleeting conviction, leaving him with just a touch of astonishment and uneasiness, that, amid the accumulation of happenstances that wove the warp and woof of the world, only the man or whatever it was that came out to repeat, nearly every night, the invariable rite for which he himself had laid down the laws, had been capable of rebelling and of creating, if only for himself, an intelligible and organized system. Something was boiling within Morvan, in contrast to the freezing cold semidarkness of the street, beyond the windowpanes, which to the eye and to the touch seemed sheets of ice. With an impetuousness that made him a little surprised at himself, he phoned the policeman at the switchboard to tell him that it wasn't worth the trouble to hunt up Lautret to take the call that he had just received, which was not at all urgent, and that he himself would see to it that he got the message when he saw him, but thinking, as he hung up again, that in any case neither he nor anyone else would see Captain Lautret until the next day, and that the only possibility of finding him before that would be to be, at eight that night, in Madame Mouton's apartment.

Despite the cold, Christmas Eve obliged people to go out on the streets, and around one o'clock, as he was slowly walking in the direction of the restaurant – he regularly went to a wine bar on the Rue León Frot or to a Chinese restaurant on the Avenue Parmentier – he could see that the Burger King on the square was packed. Whole families, loaded down with children and packages, were standing in line in front of the checkout counters or, sitting around a table on immovable benches screwed to the floor, were consuming identical menus off paper plates and out of paper cups, taking advantage of the short break in the midst of their exhausting race between reproduction and consumption. Rigorously programmed a long time before by four or five petrified institutions that complemented each other – Bank, School, Religion, Justice, Television – like a robot by virtue of the obsessive perfectionism of its assembler, their most insignificant act and most secret thought, which they were convinced were the expression of their proud individualism, find themselves repeated, identical and predictable, in each one of the strangers whom they meet on the street and who, like them, has fallen in the space of a week into debt for the entire year to come, so as to buy the same presents in the same department stores or in the same chain of shops with trademarked names, which they will deposit at the foot of the same trees decorated with little colored light bulbs, artificial snow and gold tinsel, and then sit down to eat at similar tables the same supposedly exceptional dishes to be found at the same moment on all the tables of the Western world, from which they will rise after midnight, believing themselves to be reconciled with the opaque world that shaped them, and bearing with them unto death – precisely the same for all of them – the same experiences accorded by the outside world that they are persuaded are non-transferable and unique, after having lived the same emotions and having stored in their memory the same reminiscences.

Because it was the holiday season, the owner of the Chinese restaurant on the Avenue Parmentier offered him a rice brandy when he brought him the bill: from the bottom of the little porcelain cup a naked Oriental girl in a provocative pose smiled up at him. Lifting the little cup, Morvan looked closely at the girl and had the impression that their eyes met – the brandy served as a magnifying lens – but when he looked into the bottom of the little cup once again after having downed it in one swallow, the tiny image, at once defenseless and obscene, had disappeared. As he left the restaurant, Morvan took a long, hesitant stroll before returning to the bureau. People were going and coming in all directions, loaded down with packages, entering and leaving shops, banks, bars, barber shops; not only on the avenues and on the boulevards, but also on the little side streets that ran across them, the lines of cars moved along at a crawl, piling up at the intersections, impatiently racing their motors and blowing their horns when they could go no farther. In the supermarkets, the carts filled with merchandise also gridlocked in the narrow aisles between the multicolored shelves, and collided as they approached the checkout counters. In the smaller shops, people were trying on clothes, scrutinizing the products that they were on the point of buying or went out into the street, satisfied, with their packages wrapped in gaudy paper and decorated with bright, shiny ribbons that formed multicolored spiral plumes. As on the evening before, the sky was lighter than the air, and since it was not as cold as in the morning, or gave him that impression because of the food, the brandy and the stroll, Morvan had a feeling that it would snow again. As he entered the Special Bureau, despite the fact that it was only a little after four, it was already getting dark.

Lautret had given, as they say, no sign of life all day, but this did not surprise Morvan in the least, or the police officer on guard either, for he was used to the frequent and unforeseen absences of his superiors. Two or three reporters were waiting for him in the kitchen that served as a pressroom, in which there was also a telephone, three or four straight-backed chairs, an electric coffee maker and a pile of glasses nested one inside the other, plus a wastebasket full of used cups, twisted and full of light brown coffee stains. Morvan drank a coffee with them, trying to calm them with vague promises and generalities, and then went off to shut himself up in his office. During his absence he had received an endless list of calls, from the Ministry, from the police department, from the laboratory, from two television channels, from the police captains' union. He answered two or three of them, and after looking at his wristwatch and noting that it was already six, he called Madame Mouton and told her that, inasmuch as Captain Lautret had been absent all day, he himself would come by to see her at seven-thirty. He seemed to perceive a slight disappointment in the woman's voice as she told him that she would be relieved, and also pleased, to receive him, and after hanging up he stood there for a moment reflecting on a phenomenon that had invariably attracted his attention ever since he had been a police officer, namely the well-nigh infallible instinct that frequently leads victims to take on their role with ease, not to say diligence. And at seven-thirty on the dot, he was ringing the bell at Madame Mouton's more than comfortable apartment, in the Rue Saint-Maur, some three hundred yards distant from the Special Bureau of the Crime Squad. As he waited for her to come to the door, he shook from his shoulders onto the doormat a little bit of the snow that had begun to fall once again as soon as he stepped out into the street. Despite his knowing that something horrible was in the offing, he felt, like so many other times, no emotion. He was alert, calm, clear-minded, and felt himself to be in a state of perfect physical and – I am using his own vocabulary – moral harmony.

When Madame Mouton opened the door, Morvan thought that if she had taken a while to do so it was probably because she had first gone to have one last look at herself in the mirror. Although he was not the one that she was expecting, she seemed pleasantly surprised by her police captain's physical appearance. She was doubtless over seventy and even though, despite all her efforts, she did not manage to hide her age from others, by virtue of the way she dressed and acted she gave the impression of having achieved, in her own eyes, a certain result in that sense. It struck Morvan that she must have been beautiful when she was young, and that it was not her years but, rather, the excessive efforts she took to go on looking young that ruined her appearance. He would have found her more attractive with white hair, wearing no makeup and in her bedroom slippers, reading by the fire, rather than dressed as she was to the nines, dripping with jewels, her hair dyed a reddish color and her lips and cheeks lent new life, discreetly of course, with lipstick and rouge. By the way she blinked as she opened the door, Morvan realized that in all likelihood she ordinarily wore glasses, but that she had left them inside the apartment so as to make a better impression on her visitor. Morvan acceded to this atmosphere of dissimulation, and before entering the apartment properly speaking spent a fair time inspecting the lock, which was quite ordinary, and to put the worries of the lady of the house to rest, he lied to her, assuring her that he found it quite adequate, telling himself at the same time in his heart of hearts that not one, or three, or even a thousand locks would be enough to keep her from being caught up by the hurricane that that dark presence lying curled up inside the man or whatever it was, once set in motion, raised, destroying everything in its wake. In the living room was a hearth with a fire burning brightly, and on a little low table, set between three comfortable leather armchairs, two champagne glasses as yet unfilled and several little plates filled with hors d'oeuvres. To assure her that he would be coming by the following day, Madame Mouton told Morvan, when he met her at the supermarket the day before, Captain Lautret had bought a bottle of champagne to serve for the aperitif and had given it to her, telling her to chill it so as to celebrate their meeting and the checking of the security measures, and at the same time usher out the year that was just about to end. Morvan must have thought, perhaps with irony and even with rage that, for Madame Mouton, that bottle was destined to usher out not only the year that was reaching its end, but also all of time, the fluid without substance or precise form, or a definite direction that wears away, without compassion but also without cruelty, beings and things. Morvan handed her the hat he was holding in his hand and then the overcoat from which he laboriously extracted himself. Madame Mouton left them on the armchair that would go unoccupied during their meeting and invited him to sit down in one of the two others that were still empty. Once she had seated herself opposite him, on the other side of the little low table laid out with the hors d'oeuvres, the lady of the house began to question Morvan about the crime on the Rue de la Folie Regnault, the details of which she was familiar with from the radio and television news reports, with an excessive interest, or at least so it struck Morvan, in the macabre aspects that appeared to awaken in her not so much compassion as a sort of inexplicable euphoria. Morvan found himself thinking with a certain severity that for the old woman whom he had opposite him, and who did not seem to have resigned herself yet to being an old woman, the crime wave, as they call it, could very well be no more than a pretext to drink down in her apartment that no doubt not many vigorous men visited anymore, a bottle of champagne in the company of a police official thirty years younger than herself. Since as he listened to her, Morvan, thinking of Lautret's possible arrival, looked at his wristwatch to see if it was eight o'clock yet, she interpreted his gesture as a sign of impatience, and murmuring a few polite formalities, rose from her chair and said that she was going to the kitchen to get the champagne and other things, disappearing through a door behind the armchair that Morvan was sitting in.

For a moment, only the fire in the fireplace, continuing to burn brightly, interrupted the total silence of the living room with its crackling and intermittent sputtering, until Morvan stopped listening to it and, after having sat staring at the flames, allowed his calm and attentive gaze to wander about the room. When it reached the hat and overcoat that were lying in the leather armchair, an unexpected detail attracted his attention: Madame Mouton had folded the overcoat inside out, so that a good part of the silk lining was in view, the part where the left-hand pocket was, which Morvan, who didn't smoke, never used, and indeed, almost without exaggeration, it might be said that he was even unaware of its existence. There emerged from the pocket, occupying the entire width of the aperture, the edge of a transparent plastic wrapper, so thin that it was scarcely visible, but the slight bulging of the pocket permitted one to venture the guess that it was thinner than what it contained, one of those plastic envelopes hermetically sealed by a machine that crushes the edges all the way around, compressing the contents to the maximum. Morvan did not remember having put any object whatsoever in that pocket, of whose very existence as I have just told you he was unaware, but as he rose to his feet and leaned over toward the overcoat in order to take out the plastic wrapper, he had already guessed what it contained, namely a pair of folded, flattened latex gloves, a pair of those gloves that for reasons of hygiene employees of delicatessens use to handle cold cuts, so as to separate them without spoiling them, as would happen if they used a knife and fork, and sell them to the customers. Examining them with curiosity and astonishment, he realized instantly that the man, or whatever it was, used them with the precise skill of a slaughterhouse worker so as to do his work more efficiently without leaving fingerprints. With them on, he could better handle the knife, and having once set the knife aside, open, separate, explore, tear, wrench, directly with his fingers. Those white latex hands had something in common with their victims, because the man or whatever it was could use them first in his despicable ritual until they became almost unrecognizable and then discard them. Morvan had never seen those gloves before in his life, and he deduced that someone else, someone who was laying a trap for him in order to banish his every hope, had put them in his pocket. The incredible idea occurred to him that, on receiving the overcoat from his hands, Madame Mouton had slipped, rapidly and discreetly, the gloves in the pocket, with such an abominable intent that a chaotic mixture of repulsion and rage blinded him for a moment. But almost immediately his mind became clear and alert once again, and since he heard the door of the kitchen opening at his back, he deposited the overcoat on the divan, and swiftly placed the gloves in the pocket of his suit coat.

Madame Mouton was bringing in the bottle of champagne

and some canapés of smoked salmon carefully arranged on a little plate. Morvan surreptitiously studied her without drawing any conclusion; his gaze ricocheted off this face at once ordinary and impenetrable, and yet the banal phrases uttered by the old woman all seemed to him to have more than one meaning, an implicit intent that, no matter how hard he concentrated on them, he could not manage to unveil. He wondered whether, each time that the man or whatever it was had found himself face to face with his victim, the same twofold misunderstanding had come into existence between them, for just as he could not manage to interpret the old woman's apparently banal phrases, it seemed to him that she too committed an error when she judged the man opposite her, and hence it was as though there were more than two persons in the room, the palpable presences of flesh and blood, and the senseless stylization that each of them made of the other. To tell the truth, when the knife fell, it had already been quite some time, probably from the beginning of the world on, since the annihilation had taken place. Morvan looked at the woman, trying to imagine a biography of her: she was now leaning down toward the little low table, making room for the plate with the triangular salmon canapés and he, who had stood rooted to the spot when she came back in from the kitchen, saw the fragile exposed head, the narrow shoulders, the wrinkled skin of the shrunken hand, streaked with innumerable brown veins, holding the plate, and the delicate fingers loaded with rings grasping the neck of the bottle. Her reddish hair, already a bit sparse, was divided into two symmetrical sections by a crooked white strip of scalp. After setting the plate down on the little table, Madame Mouton straightened up, attempting to hide a breathlessness that betrayed her age, and held out the bottle of champagne to Morvan to open. A slight aura of uneasiness hovered in the room: suddenly and inexplicably disconnected, the mechanism for producing fantasies which both of them possessed within themselves had stopped working, for a moment rendering unreal, not the parade of unreasonable inventions that cosmetically touched up what was outside until it took on the puerile form of their own desire, but rather, however paradoxical it may seem, the rough substance of the present in which they were incrusted, forming an indissoluble part of it, like veins in stone or knots in wood. All at once she seemed exhausted, transforming herself into the little old lady that she resisted being, and the dead years, which she had been endeavoring to ignore, suddenly piled up dizzyingly within her gaze. Morvan noted the change, thinking that perhaps it was already a late hour for her, and pretending not to have noticed anything, began opening the bottle.

Once the glasses were full, they stood toasting each other, and after taking the first sip, sat back down in the leather armchairs. Owing perhaps to those first sips of champagne, the conversation took a slightly livelier turn, and before they realized it, they had already drunk half a bottle. The mutual pretense in the beginning and the sense of unease that followed later, when she had returned from the kitchen with the bottle of champagne, gradually disappeared and a climate of trust and even of confidence set in between them. Morvan realized that the old woman was genuinely worried about all those crimes that had been committed in the neighborhood, and told himself that it must not be easy for her to come to grips with that immense gray city in which each person had to survive on his or her own, and in which, because of the isolation that it forced upon its inhabitants, and that had become a sort of norm, the very notion of society, trivialized by use, seemed to have lost all meaning. He also felt that Madame Mouton had given up her pose as a seductress, grotesque in a woman of her age, and had resigned herself to accepting the years that weighed heavily upon her, admitting the strictly professional nature of his visit. To prove to her that he would personally see to her security, Morvan put his hand in the inside pocket of his suit coat, and opening his wallet, took out a calling card that showed not only the phone numbers of the Special Bureau, but his home number as well. But when he raised his head as he was about to hand her the card, he noted that Madame Mouton was still sitting motionless in her chair, lost in thought, her eyes half closed and the nape of her neck resting against the leather back of the chair. For a few seconds, Morvan too remained motionless, with his arm halfway outstretched, the white rectangle of the card held between his thumb and forefinger, hearing in a curious distance the crackling of the fire and the old woman's regular breathing, and then, with the same slow and laborious concentration, like that of a drunk man, with which he had taken it out, he put the card back into one of the compartments of his wallet. He was on the point of folding the wallet again and placing it in his pocket when a detail on one of the bills that was protruding attracted his attention: a segment of one of those abominable oval garlands that adorned the bills in his dreams was visible near the upper corner of the real bill. The fact struck him as impossible, in violent contradiction to all logic and the enemy of all hope as well, and in order that the last vestiges of clear thought would not abandon him, he marshaled all his force of will and courage, and removing the bills, spread them out in the palm of his hand, and saw for certain that the effigies of Scylla, Charybdis, the Gorgon, the Chimera, were printed on them, and, at once threatening and distant, appeared to be disdainfully accepting the puerile homage of the gray garlands with which the crude devotion of their worshipers had adorned them. Perplexity overcame him before fear did, and before a host of dark presentiments was confirmed and the certainty of his perdition made itself entirely manifest, he found himself wandering about in the crepuscular semi-darkness, turned steel-gray by the reflection of light glancing off the snow, of the city slightly transformed by the devastating alchemy of his dream. The low temples which he was obliged to enter practically on all fours revealed the true essence of its gods, and the public monuments, blurred by the uncertainty of their ideals or by erosion, loomed up as confused forms, equestrian statues or centaurs, giant octopuses or sphinxes, angels or flesh-eating eagles, heroes or mammoths. The elongated faces of the inhabitants, gray and barely differentiated from each other, made finding one that awakened fellow-feeling, compassion, friendship or even hatred, or that simply attracted attention, a remote possibility. In that bitter semidarkness in which hours, days, weeks went by, everything seemed leveled, monotonous, resigned, and above all else useless. For the first time since he had first had that dream, Morvan realized that that city loomed up within the very depths of himself, and that from the first instant in which he had appeared in the air of this world, he had never gone beyond its walls to emerge into an improbable exterior.

Because of his having wandered about the city for so long,

heavy-hearted and perplexed, Morvan would begin to feel more and more suffocated, until he woke up, drenched with sweat but calm – the dream, despite its somber and depressing details, was not a real nightmare. In his first impressions of the waking state, surprise, not anxiety, predominated. Later on, the entire day continued to be impregnated with the moods of the dream, which gradually disappeared. That night, the same sensation of suffocating heat and pounding noises in the distance brought him back once again to the waking state. When he opened his eyes, a whitish vapor was hovering in the air in a lighted bathroom. A stream of hot water was coming out of the bathtub faucet and Morvan, kneeling down, saw that the water, as it came out of the faucet, disappeared down the drain. He rose to his feet in two stages, getting to his knees first as he leaned on the edge of the bathtub, and then standing all the way up. He was stark naked and covered with blood. The steam from the hot water fogged the surface of the mirror and Morvan, staggering a little as he tried to keep his balance, little by little saw dawning within him an idea, at once absurd and terrible, but so peremptory and growing larger and larger so swiftly that, despite the anxiety, for the first time intense, that came over him, he no longer had the slightest doubt that he was going to carry it out: it seemed to him that if he wiped away the steam covering it, the mirror would show him the image of the man or whatever it was that, for nine months now, he had been searching for. But when, with slow and clumsy movements, he turned off the faucet and wiped the mirror with the palm of his hand, despite the fact that the mirror now reflected his image, he did not recognize it as being his own. He knew that he was he, Morvan, and he knew that he was looking at the image of a man in the mirror, but the image was that of a stranger whom he was meeting for the first time in his life. Between the inside and the outside, the bridges laboriously constructed day after day, from a hesitant pale dawn to the very center of the night, had collapsed. Hurried familiar voices resounding somewhere in the house brought him out of his stupor, and when he turned around, determined to face them, and saw the movement he made to reach the door reflected, the image of the naked man looking from the mirror at his own movement seemed familiar to him once again, and the apparent fusion of the being and of his ungraspable image was once more restored.

What follows appeared in all the papers, was broadcast over all the radio stations, discussed on television, minutely analyzed in two or three hasty bestsellers, filed away in a voluminous dossier by the Crime Squad. Lautret, Combes and Juin, followed by several armed police officers, entered Madame Mouton's apartment at the very moment at which Morvan, coming from the bathroom, naked and covered with blood, entered the living room. Morvan's bare feet tripped over an object that because of the force of the collision rolled for some distance across the carpet and stopped alongside the police officers' snow-soaked shoes: Madame Mouton's head. The body lay, naked and mutilated, in the same leather armchair in which Morvan had seen her for the last time, motionless and lost in thought. A bloody disorder reigned, as they say, in the room. The bottle of champagne too had rolled across the floor, and the canapés for the aperitif, broken to pieces and trampled underfoot, were scattered all about the room as though someone had deliberately tossed them in the air. The white latex gloves and an enormous kitchen knife lay, covered with blood, on the little low table, alongside Madame Mouton's intact glass, still half full of lukewarm champagne. There was nothing in the fireplace now but a little pile of coals beneath a layer of white ashes. Morvan realized that for the entire universe the chase had reached its end, because he was too good a policeman not to know that it would be impossible to prove to the ironclad networks on the outside that perhaps they had the wrong man. Even to himself, his possible innocence was as incommunicable and remote as a memory or a dream. Vast fragments of his life escaped him, and the intimate truth of his own being was for him more ungraspable and obscure than the dark reverse side of the stars. The intense certainty of that impossibility threw to the winds the last vestiges of hope. Two or three police officers had tried to fling themselves on top of him, but Lautret had stopped them with a peremptory gesture. They all stood motionless in the room, like puppets that, because of the definite absence of the craftsman who had built them and endowed them with movement, remained rigid and frozen in actions interrupted midway, hollow simulacra made of painted cardboard: the group of police officers, with thick winter clothes still powdered with snow, assembled behind the life-size reproduction of Captain Lautret, opposite them, with one arm extended toward them, the naked bloodstained man or whatever it was, and in the background, sprawled out on the leather armchair, the headless mannequin hacked to pieces, whose false plastic organs, red, greenish and blue, could be glimpsed though exaggeratedly gaping gashes, puppets more exterior, accidental and lifeless than the black, gelid element from whose bosom they had unexpectedly emerged, and which, sooner or later, for no particular reason, will resorb them. It was Morvan who made the first move: picking up the head, he sought Lautret's eyes to try to discover signs of his victory in them, but, disappointed and confused, he discerned only compassion.

In twenty-four hours, the crisis cell presided over by the Prefect, but in reality directed by Lautret, and made up of magistrates, forensic physicians, police officers and psychiatrists, put the puzzle together and drafted a first press bulletin. In the weeks that followed, each one of the details was minutely analyzed: for a couple of months, a confidential report on Morvan had been circulating among the senior officers of the police force. Naturally it occurred to no one that he might be the author of the endless series of crimes, but serious suspicions as to his mental health did exist. His solitary ways and his taciturn temperament had become exacerbated after his separation, and above all after his father's suicide, and it was evident that his depressive tendencies had grown worse in recent months. Moreover, and that was what was most worrisome, a number of police officers had happened to meet him on the street during his nocturnal wanderings and had noted his vacant stare, so much like that of a sleepwalker that he had passed by them without recognizing them. Two or three times he had entered the Special Bureau early in the morning without looking at anyone, as though he were sleepwalking, and had proceeded to shut himself up in his room till the next morning. In reality, the letter from the Ministry dealt, in veiled language, with Morvan, and since Lautret, who spoke up in Morvan's defense to his superiors, had realized what was going on, he had ostentatiously torn the letter to bits in the presence of his colleagues so as to demonstrate publicly, but not in an explicit way, his loyalty to his friend. Lautret was convinced, moreover, that Morvan – such was his trust in the latter's perspicacity – suspected what sort of plot was being hatched against him.

On the night of Madame Mouton's murder, Lautret, who had forgotten that he had promised to visit her, came back to the Special Bureau around ten-thirty and learned from the police officer on duty of the call from the old woman. He decided to telephone her to apologize, and since she didn't answer, he began to worry, to the point that he rounded up his men and rushed to the Rue Saint-Maur. Since no one came to the door, they forced it open. That was how they surprised Morvan coming, naked and covered with blood, out of the bathroom alongside Madame Mouton's mutilated corpse. Morvan's fingerprints were all over the apartment, and even on Madame Mouton's glass, and they discovered that, in order to make his work easier, he had put sleeping powder in her champagne. They had found some in Madame Mouton's glass, but in the dregs left in the overturned bottle there were no traces of any. The knife came from the kitchen. Since there were no traces either of sperm or of rape on the victim's body, as there had been in all the other cases, and since this was the first instance in which a drug had been used to put her to sleep, in the first hours of the investigation Lautret maintained that Morvan might have committed that one crime in a fit of dementia, but Combes and Juin, whom he sent to search Morvan's apartment, came back with a bunch of twenty-eight keys – all of them fitting the locks of the apartments where crimes had been committed – and a packet of a hundred pairs of latex gloves, from which exactly twenty-nine were missing. As far as the police and justice were concerned, the case was closed. When the moment arrived to face public opinion, Lautret asked to be relieved, but his request was refused, so that for a week he appeared on all the news broadcasts on television and on the radio, explaining the details of the case to the public. The moment he was free, he went off to shut himself up in Caroline's apartment.

Though less glorious, Morvan's fame surpassed the police captain's. A blurred photograph of him, spread over several columns, adorned the front page of the papers. A reporter had the idea of calling him *the monster of la Bastille*, and almost immediately all the others adopted the nickname, writing page after page about Morvan, about whom they really knew almost nothing, turning him, at least for a month, into one of the biggest celebrities in the country, if not on the entire continent, and if we wish to come close to the truth, in the whole world. The tabloids accused him of cannibalism and ended up pinning on him, by means of tortuous speculations, a number of crimes that had gone unsolved. There were no demonstrations in favor of lynching him, because that's not how the public goes about things there, but in private, in the solitude of their bedroom suites bought on credit and their souvenirs brought back from vacations in the Balearics, Turkey or the Riviera, each one of the television viewers or the readers of magazines with feature stories recounting the private lives of politicians, of football players, of de luxe whores and of the English royal family, in the tumult of their crude emotions as ephemeral as will-o-the-wisps, had already put his head on the block and let the guillotine blade fall a thousand times. But infamy in capital letters, though it is of course intolerable, has as its main characteristic fleetingness, the consequence of a lack of desire to see things through, which assures its victims of a prompt and certain oblivion. Morvan was not even grazed by this spectacular renown, because from the moment that he came out of the bathroom, naked and bloodstained, he fell into a profound state of self-absorption. When Captain Lautret went over to him and gently urged him to get dressed and accompany him to the Special Bureau, Morvan shook his head several times and gave a sarcastic little laugh that Lautret knew to be typical of him and that in general expressed in his case a feeling of obviousness when confronted with a well-reasoned argument or a curious but incontrovertible fact. Although Lautret and the other police officers, who gazed at him in stupefaction, did not know it, the ineluctable fact on which Morvan was reflecting as he started to get dressed was his conviction that even though it would be impossible for him to prove his innocence in the outside world, it would be even more difficult for him to prove it to himself, and though no empirical residuum of his acts remained in his memory, he would never be able to be certain that he had not committed them, just as, conversely, many others of which he had apparently real memories, once they had been diluted in the sea of events that occur, no one, himself least of all, could be certain that they had really taken place. Now that everything seemed to indicate that he was the one who had committed atrocious crimes, the anguished sensation of proximity of that destructive shadow had disappeared, and instead of overwhelming him, the banishing of all hope, both contradictory and benevolent, relieved him. When he had finished dressing, accompanied by Lautret and a pair of police officers – the others stayed behind to record mere facts and evidence – he docilely allowed himself to be driven to the Special Bureau, his eyes fixed on the midnight snow whose flakes came crashing into the windshield of the car.

From that moment on, and for weeks, he stopped speaking, having realized that, in the material net into which he had fallen, words served no purpose. At the endless interrogation sessions he sometimes answered with a movement of his head, or with an excessive facial expression in slow motion, such as, for example, opening his eyes and his mouth as wide as he could, and without this movement of his head or this facial expression having anything whatsoever to do with the question; sometimes he would answer just one question with a movement of his head that began as an assent and ended as a denial, and even with a movement that was affirmative and negative at the same time, and that because of this combination of opposite meanings ended up being vaguely circular. Every so often, there again appeared the pensive, sarcastic little laugh, which, instead of causing the interrogations to make headway, bogged them down, because that secret, self-satisfied conviction that the little laugh seemed to reveal was like a smooth steel wall interposed between him and the universe, so that after a few days the police officers and the examining magistrates, exhausted, gave in to the insistent pressure of Captain Lautret and turned him over to the psychiatrists.

Because of a professional bias, police officers perhaps tend to overestimate the importance of dissimulation, and psychiatrists that of dementia. A third explanation, like everything that has no name, strikes them as unacceptable. Hence, within a short time it was established as certain fact that the monster of la Bastille, as they called him, was, as they say, a schizophrenic. With Caroline's help and even Lautret's, inasmuch as the psychiatrists were unable to get a word out of Morvan, despite the fact that he docilely agreed to take all sorts of written tests, they were able to reconstitute his clinical history and explain the reasons for his behavior. Caroline recounted in detail the life they had led in common for years. According to her, Morvan was a generous and solicitous man, yet taciturn and distant. He had had that sort of sleepwalking attack sporadically in recent years, and shortly before the separation these episodes had become more frequent. But since in general they happened in his sleep, she had thought that it was a case of ordinary somnambulism. Only once had she seen him get out of bed, get dressed, and go out onto the street in that state. Since she had heard people say that it could be dangerous for a sleepwalker to be suddenly awakened, she had followed him down the street for a good half-hour. Morvan was walking a bit more stiffly than usual, but was behaving like a normal person. On returning to the house, he had opened the locked door with a key, undressed, and climbed back into bed. According to Caroline, he remembered nothing the following day, but had told her about a strange dream he'd had, having to do with a stroll in an unknown, yet at the same time familiar, city. The psychiatrists told her that certain types of schizophrenia result in a split personality, and the acts that the subject performs during the period in which the split is total never reach the conscious level, his consciousness being entirely absorbed in a delirious fantasy that blocks out all representations that have an empirical origin. According to the psychiatrists, it was quite possible that, owing to strong pressure from his guilt feelings, from the very moment at which the impulse to kill came over him, the delirious fantasy, very much like the lack of consciousness of a sleepwalker who is sound asleep yet at the same time capable of carrying out acts without committing errors in the empirical domain, took over in his consciousness for the duration of his acts, with the result that neither before, nor during, nor afterwards, was Morvan aware of the crimes he committed. Thanks to his family history, it was relatively easy for the psychiatrists to explain the cause of those crimes. Abandoned by his mother after his birth, Morvan was a rather sad child, and however great the affective support of his father, it was not sufficient to consolidate his mental equilibrium: he acquired a slightly dissociated personality, along with a strong sense of responsibility, owing perhaps to a guilt complex over the disappearance of his mother, who, according to his father's first version, which Morvan had often heard when he was a youngster, had died in childbirth, that is to say because of his birth. Morvan must have instinctively had his doubts about his father's version, and his penchant for resolving criminal enigmas might well have stemmed from the unconscious certainty that there were mysterious elements in his own childhood. As proof of his dissociated personality, the psychiatrists put forward Caroline's confidential assertion that Morvan's sex life was rather impoverished and conventional. As the years passed, his criminal investigations gradually came to be his sole interest, and since he was not unaware of his own shortcomings, he himself had decided to separate so as to give Caroline back her freedom.

That separation brought on, according to the psychiatrists, the catastrophe. When he heard the news, Morvan's father, who had kept the secret for more than forty years, thought that it was the weight of that secret that was destroying the life of his son, toward whom he had felt a sense of responsibility, not only in later years, but from the very first, for not having been able to keep his wife. He too felt guilty, and the story was repeated, so that he decided, before taking his life, to tell Morvan the truth. On his return from the old people's home, Morvan had recounted the story to Caroline, telling her that, after the forty years that had gone by, his mother's attitude was a matter of indifference to him. According to the psychiatrists, that apparent indifference was a way of fighting against the aggressive instincts that had always been latent in him, as was proved by his sexual conduct and his separation, but that were now beginning to be reactivated. His father's suicide had unleashed his hatred toward everything feminine.

Twenty-nine innocent old women – according to the term employed by the psychiatrists, who, once they had proved their ability to use the vocabulary of their profession, which they call scientific, always allowed themselves certain rhetorical liberties – twenty-nine innocent old women were his surrogate victims. In each of them, Morvan saw the mother who had abandoned him. With great perspicacity, the psychiatrists point out in their report that all the old women were around seventy-five years old, the approximate age of Morvan's mother if she were still alive. A strict, and naturally symbolic, ritual ruled over, as the saying goes, the murders. Morvan had to present himself to the little old women in the sincere belief that, as head of the Special Bureau, his sole concern was to protect them. A stage of mutual seduction was established, according to the psychiatrists, between him and the old women. Again according to the psychiatrists, there was an evident erotic aspect in those relations, although neither Morvan nor the little old women were for the most part really aware of it. Morvan convinced them to keep their relations secret so as not to alert the murderer, thereby giving them the illusion that they were participating in the police investigation. And if the old women fell into the trap so easily, it was thanks to Morvan's official authority, which made them feel that they were being protected, and to the fact that he was a man at the height of his physical vigor, thus awakening in them, by virtue of that protective intimacy, sensations that had long since been forgotten. In certain cases, they had even acceded voluntarily, in a sudden rejuvenation, to sexual congress, before the ceremony properly speaking, whereby they felt safeguarded precisely because they were in the company of Morvan, took place. That ceremony, apparently so cruel, had its own logic, according to the psychiatrists, and seen through the eyes of science, according to them, it made much more sense than it appeared to: in their report they interpreted everything as the result of a love-hate relation toward the image of the mother. The tortures, for example, were not inflicted out of sheer sadism, but with the aim, rather, of verifying whether that body exterior to his own, from which he had been expelled, was as sensitive to pain as his own body, and the various mutilations, decapitations, quartering, thoracic or abdominal slashings, as well as the habit of poking about, piercing the viscera, the eyes, the tongue, the ears, etc., an attempt to penetrate – I do not know if the word was deliberately chosen by those who drafted the report – the supposed mystery of the maternal body, and also perhaps the reason for which that body, disappeared without a trace at the very instant that he had come into the light of day of this world, according to the psychiatrists, had allowed itself to be fecundated in order to engender him, feed him, keep him warm and protected for nine months, and then drop him, unfinished and bloody, abandoning him once and for all. The rapes *pre* and *post mortem* were also, according to the psychiatrists, a symptom of ambivalence, demonstrating his sexual desire toward his mother, and in a footnote, in an extrascientific tone, of the philosophic-aphoristic type, rather, the report notes that that instinctive, insane love for the mother who had abandoned him, like the trust in and the erotic attraction of the old women for their torturer, tended to demonstrate that, beyond what Oscar Wilde, whose name is cited in full in the report, said, human beings not only destroy what they love, but above all love what destroys them. If Captain Lautret and the other police officers from the Special Bureau had not caught him, Morvan would have been able to prolong his series of crimes to infinity, with the same regularity and at an even swifter pace, up to several a day, in accordance with the urgency of his impulses, and in the report the psychiatrists compared Morvan's dementia to a mechanical device built to carry out a single movement and doomed to repeat it time and time again until the wear and tear on the material and the definite breakdown of the mechanism kept it from doing so, without the remotest possibility of escaping from this scheme of things. Since there was no consciousness of the act, there could be neither modification nor abandonment nor repentance. So long as his arm had the strength to rise and fall as it brandished the knife, according to the psychiatrists, it would do so indefinitely in the presence of an old woman, without hesitation and without remorse. Hence, even though they unanimously agreed that he was not responsible in the eyes of the law, they strongly recommended to the authorities that Morvan be sent to a mental asylum and confined to an individual cell in, despite his apparent docility, the ward for the violently insane. The psychiatrists appeared to regard Morvan as one of those objects which, through ignorance of their contents, their mechanism and their use, are considered dangerous, and out of mistrust are therefore best kept isolated.

This isolation did not seem to perturb Morvan to any great degree. After a few months, he began to speak again. It is true that he did not say very much, but at least when he was asked a question, he offered a precise answer, in a monosyllable if possible, and if he needed something, he asked for it in a direct, amiable and natural way. From the physical point of view, confinement also appeared to have done him good: he had a keen appetite, and though he refused to receive visitors, he willingly accepted the packages of food and clothing that Caroline regularly sent him. He seemed to be more impassive than serene and very careful of his personal hygiene and appearance, so that among the madmen in the asylum, he always attracted visitors' attention, because he was clean, carefully shaven and impeccably dressed, to the point that many of the visitors mistook him for a member of the staff, and sometimes even went so far as to ask him for information that Morvan promptly and courteously supplied, and it was never wrong. Although it beggars belief, the state, thanks to the intercession of certain colleagues of his, gave him a disability pension, so that he even had a bank account which, inasmuch as he spent almost nothing, brought him very good interest. Every day, accompanied by two male nurses, two men who looked neither more nor less vigorous than he, he went out for a run of several kilometers around the sports arena of the institution. When he went to the dispensary to have routine clinical tests, the physician on duty, as he auscultated him or took his blood pressure, shook his head and laughed, saying that, with health like his, Morvan would probably bury all his acquaintances. Raising his naked, muscular torso which the doctor checked by leaning his ear against his skin or by tapping him lightly here and there with his knuckles, Morvan gave, though the doctor, who believed him to be almost catatonic, never once noticed, a very slight smile that showed more in his eyes than on his lips, revealing an enigmatic pride.

One day he telephoned Caroline and asked her to send him his old illustrated mythology book, a present which his father had brought him at his grandmother's house one time when he came back from one of his trips and which he had kept ever since, and also the copies of all the documents concerning the first twenty-seven crimes, which he had taken the precaution of storing away in his apartment, and told her to go ask Combes, not Lautret, for a photocopy of the last two. Caroline brought him the package herself, but Morvan refused to accept it from her, limiting himself to having one of the guards hand her a friendly though impersonal note. When he finally had the rather bulky package in hand, he looked at it with satisfaction but left it on the table for several days without opening it. One night he finally undid, patiently and skillfully, the triple or quadruple knot with which the package was tied and without even taking a glance at the police dossiers, took out, with evident pleasure, the book of mythology, the back of which was torn and the pages now a himself on his bed, he began to leaf through it, not reading the text printed in big letters meant for a young reader, but lingering with profound interest over the old colored illustrations showing the fall of Troy, Orestes upon his return home, Tantalus serving the gods his own children as food, Ulysses tied to the mast of his boat with his ears stopped up so as not to hear, for fear of succumbing to their spell, the song of the sirens, and also Scylla and Charybdis, the Gorgon, the Chimera, and above all the unbearably white bull, with horns in the shape of a half-moon, eternally raping in Crete, beneath a plane tree, after having abducted her on a beach in Tyre or Sidon, the terrified nymph. The pile of police records appeared to be forgotten on the table. Fleetingly raising his head, Morvan glanced at them as if to assure himself that they were still there, but immediately losing interest again became absorbed in contemplation of the colored illustrations. In any event, he now knew that harsh time, from that calm night onward, was finally about to be on his side.

Despite the fact that he has been listening to him with rapt attention, when Pigeon stops talking and rivets on him a pleased and expectant gaze, Tomatis stirs a little in his white wrought iron chair, and avoiding Pigeon's gaze, allows his own to wander for a few seconds and then, at precisely the moment that his eyes grow calm, his entire body ceases to move as his shoulder, where the cloth of his sweat-drenched blue shirt is plastered to his skin, comes to rest against the back of the chair. An expression, bordering on the comical because of the mistrust and mental effort that it connotes, appears on his face, and Soldi, equidistant from the two of them, observes that when Pigeon's eyes glimpse Tomatis's expression they light up, discreetly, with a wicked gleam.

expression they light up, discreetly, with a wicked gleam.

"It's possible," Tomatis says ill-humoredly, lost in thought, and then absent-mindedly raises his hand to the left pocket of his shirt and takes out a cigar case of stiff dark leather, whose grooved shape, formed by three long parallel cylindrical compartments, reveals its capacity. With the same impatient and distracted air, Tomatis opens the case, pushes part way out of it a medium-sized cigar wrapped in cellophane, and knowing beforehand that neither of the two will accept, offers it first to Soldi and then to Pigeon. Without even waiting for them to explicitly refuse it, he takes it out of the case, and after closing the case and putting it back in the pocket of his shirt, leaning once again against the white wrought iron chair back, begins to twirl the cigar in his apparently distracted fingers, and then, beginning to remove it from its cellophane wrapper, repeats, this time looking Pigeon straight in the eye:

"It's possible."

The wicked gleam in Pigeon's eyes – on noting it Tomatis smiles in turn, as does Soldi, like three little lights turned on in the night, in the distance, not simultaneously and intensely however, but, rather, successively and discreetly – descends to his lips which, only slightly parted, quiver slightly.

"It's possible," Tomatis says for a third time. "But why make everything so complicated? In physics or mathematics, the simplest solution is always the best one, and in addition, as experts of that sort say – and you should see the way they dress – the most elegant."

Aware of having caught the attention of his audience, Tomatis stops speaking and unhurriedly devotes himself to lighting his cigar. Pigeon, who has seen him smoke them since adolescence, knows that the task always takes him a long while, but that this time he will make it even more prolonged than usual. Moreover, the cigar that Tomatis has taken out of the case is a Havana, a Romeo y Julieta, of medium thickness, a box of twenty-five costing sixty-eight dollars, and if Pigeon is right on the mark with regard to the price it is because he is the one who bought it at the duty-free shop in the Paris airport, a couple of minutes before boarding the plane. Almost at the very instant that the trip was decided on, the image of himself buying the box of cigars for Tomatis, and the image of Tomatis receiving it from him have been a sort of pleasant anticipated memory, an experience lived intensely before the deadly talons of what is actually occurring seize it, trivialize it and then dump it, without rage or remorse, into the dustbin of oblivion. Tomatis rummages in his trousers pocket in search of a box of wooden matches, and when he finally comes across it, he takes it out with ceremonious slowness and places it on the table. While he is about it, to make the sense of expectation last a little longer still, he raises the cigar to his right ear and squeezes it several times with his fingertips to check whether it still has the requisite moistness, a completely superfluous operation inasmuch as Pigeon has heard him say, time and again, *ad nauseam* one might say, that cigars bought at airports, being poorly stored, are almost without exception too dry, and then, opening the box of matches, he takes one out, and with the end opposite the little inflammable red head, perforates the rounded end of the cigar, which he immediately raises to his mouth, and without letting go of it, begins licking it and twirling it around between his lips so as to moisten it properly. Pigeon notes that even though Tomatis's fingertips and the

palm of his hand are a bit lighter, the backs of his fingers and
the skin of his neck and face are almost the same color as the
cigar. Tomatis finally leaves off licking it, examines with
exaggerated attentiveness the moistened end, and seems to
have made up his mind to light it, although so slowly that
the match that he has used to perforate the end of it, which
he is still holding in his left hand, and the box which, after
having placed the cigar between his lips once again, he has
picked up from the table with his right hand, search each
other out in the air in zigzagging, discontinuous passes, their
movement through space so unfunctional that they are
reminiscent of some sort of anomaly of coordination,
capturing Soldi's and Pigeon's attention to such a point that,
having forgotten even the purpose of this long delay, they
follow, impatiently and intently, the imaginary labyrinth that
the movements trace in the air. And yet, when the match
finally meets the little brown strip of sandpaper on the box,
one energetic pass across it is enough to cause its little red
head to burst into flame, and cupping the palm of his hand
to protect it, Tomatis conscientiously applies it to the end of
the cigar, meanwhile breathing in until the entire circular
surface has lighted up. Tomatis removes the cigar from his
mouth, examines the lighted end, and immediately after
checking the result of the operation, finding it satisfactory,
drops on to the ground, not even shaking it to put it out, the
little match head that is still alight when it disappears
underneath the table. Several deep puffs, his eyelids half closed
because of the gaze fixed watchfully on the lighted end, return
to the night air thick streams of smoke that are straight and
heavy as they come out from between his lips and become
tenuous and arborescent as they begin to disperse. Although

he has made all his dilatory gestures with a serious, almost solemn, expression, when he decides that it is time to put an end to them, even before raising his eyelids to meet the gaze of his two conversational partners, Tomatis gives a quick guffaw, a sort of private laugh with which he mocks his own meticulous slowness, revealing at the same time its purely theatrical nature.

"The other," he says, turning serious once again, removing the cigar from his mouth and pointing the burning circular end at Pigeon's chest. "His old friend. And out of sheer pleasure, because he enjoyed making little old women suffer, raping them, torturing them and killing them. Out of sheer pleasure. He liked to make them believe that he had come to protect them, and garnered a supplementary enjoyment from their terror when they recognized the trap they'd fallen into. Anyway, thanks to the fact that everyone knew him because he often appeared on television, he was the only one who had the possibility of going on doing what he was doing. When they recognized him, they believed him immediately and let him into their apartments without the slightest suspicion. Naturally it excited him to fan their illusion, to revive their last feeble sparks of hope, and then, with a brusque, unexpected gesture, do them in. And all this without a split personality or anything like it: perfectly lucid and pleased with himself, proudly claiming for himself, merely on account of the legitimacy of his impulses, the right to dupe, to rape, to torture, to kill. He counted on two high cards in order to do so, his vocation and his easy access to them, and as the corpses piled up, on a third card, the voluptuous thrill of the risk.

The circle, however, was narrowing. He enjoyed

performing a balancing act on the tightrope, but he was not unaware of the yawning abyss below. Since he was a close friend of the man who was directing the search, he knew that, even if officially no new fact brought any progress, Morvan's presentiments took into account the proximity, even the familiarity, of the beast. And the beast knew that on the day it was caught, the hunter could be no one else save Morvan. Morvan, whom he truly admired and to whom he owed everything, two more than sufficient reasons to also feel a twinge of hatred for him. Moreover, his friend's wife was not indifferent to him. If he shuffled the cards in precisely the right way, he would win across the board.

Long before the crimes began, he learned from Morvan's wife of the crises that he was going through. And after their separation and the suicide of Morvan's father, when he began to court her openly, she told him the story of the mother who had abandoned him the day that he was born so as to go off with a member of the Gestapo. Long before wanting to charge him with the crimes, in order to make him give up his post as head of the Special Bureau and thereby take his place, not only out of ambition, but also because if he himself headed the investigations he would never be discovered, he began, discreetly, using third parties, to circulate rumors about Morvan's mental health. Morvan did not know that the letter from the Ministry referred, in veiled terms, to these rumors. The other had laid no groundwork other than to take his place at the bureau and in the marriage bed, and only shortly thereafter, and little by little, did the idea take shape that he could also, while still playing the same game, charge him with all his crimes.

Although he had shuffled the cards several weeks before,

and begun his maneuvering a little while before, the first hand that would force Morvan to enter the game was played out in his own office, when he tore up the letter from the Ministry. At that moment, he had already premeditated and begun to lay the foundation for what would be, at least for quite a good while, his last two crimes. As other people have several bank accounts, which they use only in case of necessity, he had several old women in reserve. That same morning he waited until Madame Mouton went out to do her shopping, followed her, and pretended to have met her by chance at the supermarket. Knowing that he would not be at the bureau, he told her to phone him there the next morning to confirm their engagement that night, and in case he wasn't in, to ask to speak with Captain Morvan. In order to be certain that he or Morvan would turn up at her apartment as planned, and making as if the idea had occurred to him at that moment, he took another bottle of champagne from the shelf and told her that, when they left the supermarket, after he'd paid for it, he would give it to her for her to put in the refrigerator, so that they could drink it together when they saw each other the following day. He needed two bottles for his plan, but he had brought the first one to the supermarket himself, after having opened it at his apartment the night before, putting a sleeping powder in it and then carefully closing it again. He paid for both bottles, gave Madame Mouton the one with the sleeping powder in it, and put the other away until the following night.

In order for the plan to be carried out, Morvan had to be certain that the other man was the one he was searching for. So the other tore up the letter and threw the pieces in the air, knowing that Morvan, so meticulous by nature, would put them together, since it was an official document that he had no copy of, but he took the precaution of keeping one little bit of paper himself. A little later, after having slit the old lady of the Rue de la Folie Regnault open from the throat to the pubis with the knife, he took a shower as usual, dressed carefully, and before going out, taking with him key number twenty-eight, he left the little piece of paper on the wall-to-wall carpet, in full view, so that no police officer, least of all Morvan, could fail to note its presence. Even though Morvan did not personally open the door, in any event the little piece of paper would be handed over to him. But once again he was in luck, because it was Morvan himself who found it. That minuscule bit of paper, of no consequence for anyone else, signifying nothing, worth nothing, symbolizing nothing, would for Morvan be the root, the trunk and the shiny branches of evidence. The other knew that he would discount Combes and Juin, and draw the inevitable conclusion, but since that little piece of paper did not constitute proof for anyone but Morvan, he would not say a word to anyone until he was able to produce irrefutable proof of his certainty. The other had already slipped into Morvan's office and tucked the latex gloves in the pocket of his overcoat. He wanted Morvan to find the gloves at some point, not only because he had decided to fabricate concrete proofs, but also because he wanted Morvan, on account of his fits of somnambulism, to begin to have suspicions concerning his own guilt.

He knew that the phone call from Madame Mouton would be a new element that would serve to confirm Morvan's suspicions, and that Morvan would go in person to wait for him at the apartment before eight o'clock, if only, even though he had no proof against him, to prevent him from committing another crime. He had calculated that the effect of the dose of sleeping powder he had put in the champagne would last for two to three hours. When Morvan saw that the bills that he had in his wallet were identical to the ones in his dream, he was already starting to drop off to sleep, and the pensive expression on Madame Mouton's face, as she sat motionless in her armchair with her eyes half-closed, was also an effect of the sleeping powder. The other entered the apartment at eight-thirty and found them both asleep. He stripped Morvan naked, decapitated Madame Mouton on top of Morvan's body so that her blood would spatter all over him, and also put the latex gloves on him so as to leave his fingerprints on them and then took them off, and for the same reason he put Morvan's fingers in contact with the bunch of keys and the packet of gloves from which twenty-nine pairs were missing. Then he replaced the bottle of champagne with the one that had no sleeping powder in it, sent it rolling across the floor, making sure that a little bit of champagne was left in the bottom of the bottle to be compared with that in Madame Mouton's glass, washed Morvan's glass, broke it, and finally carried Morvan to the bathroom naked and left him there on the floor. Then he washed himself, got dressed, put the bottle with the sleeping powder and his own latex gloves in a plastic bag, carefully wrapped up the packet of gloves and the bunch of keys, opened the hot water faucet so that Morvan would have the impression that he had awakened in the middle of an act begun in a somnambulistic state, and left the apartment. From there he went directly to Morvan's apartment, where he left the packet of gloves and the bunch of keys, went downstairs to the street, got rid of the plastic bag containing

the bottle and his own gloves, and headed for the Special
Bureau. He had calculated how long the effect of the sleeping
powder would last, and if possible, he wanted to arrive at the
apartment with the other police officers just as Morvan began
to wake up. He phoned a couple of times, knowing that.
even if he were awake Morvan would not answer, and then,
taking with him a large group of police officers who would
serve as irrefutable witnesses, he set out for Madame Mouton's
apartment. It made little difference whether Morvan was
awake or asleep, since all the bureau chiefs knew about his
somnambulistic crises, and Caroline would be obliged to
testify as to what she had told him regarding them, but once
again the cards were in his favor, because just as they forced
the door open, Morvan, who was still half asleep from the
sedative but thought for a few seconds that he was now awake,
failed to recognize his own image in the mirror and came out
of the bathroom, naked and covered with blood, stumbling
over the head of Madame Mouton and sending it rolling
across the rug as far as the police officers' snow-soaked shoes.
The police officers were about to fling themselves on top of
him, but the other stopped them: he wanted Morvan to have
time to reason, to analyze the situation, the concrete evidence,
the number and the credibility of the witnesses, and reach by
himself the conclusion that he was doomed. More than that:
after certainty, he wanted doubt too to get its share of the
pot, and wanted Morvan himself, even though he had no
memory of it, and even if he did it might not have proved
anything either, to admit the possibility that he himself was
the mortal shadow that he had been chasing for nine months.
The other already knew that, having analyzed the facts,
Morvan would be unable to accuse him, since this accusation

would be for the witnesses and for the examining magistrates an additional proof of perversity and dementia. When Morvan began to seek his eyes, the other realized that the game was over, and then and there, knowing that he could gain an advantage even from that, deigned to show compassion.

Because of the effort that his words have required of him, and perhaps because of the effects of the cigar as well, which he has been taking deep puffs on at the most intense moments of his monologue, when Tomatis falls silent, his forehead continues to break out in sweat, and the drops slide down along the loose folds of his wrinkled, suntanned face. When he leans slightly forward in his chair and, picking up his glass once again, takes a swallow of now-lukewarm beer, because of the temperature of the beverage his air of satisfaction is briefly clouded by an expression of displeasure. The others too, even though they have been listening to him without moving, are sweating quite heavily, and like him, are aware of their shirts plastered to the skin of their shoulders. Once they have gotten out of the motorboat at the Yacht Club, after taking their leave of the deck hand, they have decided to have dinner in the patio in which they are now sitting – a beer garden, they call it in the city – but before that Soldi has taken each of them home in the car so as to allow them to rest a little and take a shower, and they have joined each other again around nine-thirty. Alicia and "the little Frenchman", who have not opened their mouths during the ride in the car, but who, on separating outside Héctor's studio, where Pigeon is staying, have planned something together in a low voice as though they were a pair of conspirators, and as though they would have liked to keep at all costs their distance from the discouraging world of the grown-ups, have not even deigned to answer Tomatis's and Pigeon's invitation to join them for dinner, so that after nine o'clock, having each arrived on his own, proceeding from different places in the city, which already lay in darkness, the three of them, freshly bathed and changed, hungry and thirsty, and above all eager to go on talking together, have met in the patio illuminated by the strings of lights hanging from the white walls, the branches of the giant acacias and the palm trees. To have more peace and quiet, they have purposely chosen the table farthest away from the entrance, and sat down while not too many people have arrived yet, Tomatis with his back to the entrance, where the bar, the barbecue and the kitchen are being set up against a brick wall painted white and covered over by a single straw roof, with Pigeon opposite him, so that he has passed the time watching the barman and the cooks, and the bustling back and forth of the waiters along the red paths of powdered brick as they serve the tables scattered among the trees, and with Soldi equidistant from the two of them, at the head of the table, seeing the whole time, beyond the cart wheels, each of a different size, painted white, the little enclosure of white balustrades, and the dark street, the low building of the bus terminal which, although it was officially opened twenty years before, Pigeon still calls the new terminal. The three of them have residua of the sensations they have experienced throughout the hot, brightly sunlit day, and the boat trip on the river, the visit to Rincón Norte, the tangled network of islands with washed-out colors and of water will surely leave each of the three of them with his own memories, its source a common experience, yet impossible to translate into the private languages of the others, which will accompany them till they die. They have returned to the city amid the sounds of nightfall in the background, and the quick shower they have taken has brought them only temporary refreshment, a momentary, superficial relief. Conversation alone has made them forget for a few hours the mind-numbing heat, the disquieting, dark time that traverses them, continuous and unbroken, like a constant, monotonous background accompaniment. Alert and voluble, serious and playful, their attention narrowly focused yet at the same time free, for a couple of hours they have obliged the forces exerting their pull toward darkness to remain outside their lives, while at the same time never ceasing for a moment to know that, all around, close at hand, ready as always to carry them off, those forces still palpitate.

Now that Tomatis has stopped talking, Soldi thinks that the self-satisfied air that he assumes is more feigned than genuine, and for a minute at least, the three of them remain silent. It is a silence that is thoughtful yet slightly uncomfortable, as though a feeling of embarrassment had overcome them, which Soldi, who nonetheless is beginning to feel it too, finds inexplicable. The three shirts – the blue one, the yellow one and the bright green, almost fluorescent, one – that two hours ago were clean, stiff and well-ironed, but are now limp with sweat, remain motionless, as do the tanned faces and arms protruding from their collars and sleeves. A ballerina, gone astray in the night air, far from the lights strung between the trees, around which thousands and thousands of its fellow creatures whirl and collide, flutters in the emptiness above the table, above the glasses and the dirty dishes, amid remains of the meal, olive pits, tired, twisted quarters of lemon, scattered bread crumbs, oil, grease, cheese turned hard, bits of tomato. The butterfly circles, fluttering the whitish wings that become almost transparent, flying lower and lower over the remains of the meal, as though it found it hard to fly higher, and as though the weight of what is impelling it downward, furious at not having been able as yet to attract the three men who remain silently seated around the table, were venting its wrath upon it. The three of them begin to watch it with interest and a certain surprise, they see it loop dizzily back and forth upon itself, rise, descend, in narrower and narrower circles, until, exhausted, it falls, like a little white stone, straight into the plate of olives. Pigeon bends down toward it, and shaking a threatening forefinger above the dish, says to it in a reproving tone of voice:

"I warned you when I had to take you out of my pocket that we didn't want to see any more of you around here."

"It's not the same one," Tomatis says, leaning over the dish of olives.

"You never know," Pigeon says. "And anyway, what's the difference?"

The little white body flutters more and more slowly, half submerged in what is left of the oil. The few olives still on the plate, ovoid shapes of a dark, lustrous green, appear, alongside the little whitish spot, to be in the throes of death, more mysterious and mineral than the pyramids, and muter, more distant, more disdainful than the stars. When the butterfly stops moving altogether, a violent, unexpected clap of thunder that lingers on in the night, making it vibrate, gives the impression of shaking the branches of the trees and all the ambient air, for a sudden gusting wind begins to blow. Tomatis points with what remains of his cigar at the butterfly, motionless now in the middle of the pool of oil, and then points the glowing end at the sky above.

"Its sixth hour," he says.

"Not even," Pigeon says. "It's a coincidence."

A blue flash of lightning that will bring in its wake another clap of thunder illuminates the patio. Overhead, the plumes of the palm trees and the branches of the acacias are whipped violently back and forth, their movements bringing down the strings of lights hanging from them and producing an agitated back-and-forth of lights and shadows, and though the paper tablecloths on the abandoned tables begin to fly through the air and the brick dust to form reddish whirlwinds in the air above the paths down which waiters and customers alike excitedly dash, Tomatis and Pigeon remain sitting at the table without moving, leaning over the dish of olives. Soldi observes them, curious and surprised: closer to fifty than to forty, they do not appear to be unaware of what is approaching, and yet they give the impression of being as firmly settled in the present as on an indestructible throne. They seem to be hoping for nothing, desiring nothing. Indifferent to the chaos all about them, they sit motionless gazing at the plate of olives, with no particular expression denoting in their sun-darkened faces any sort of emotion or thought. Self-forgetful, they appear to have decided, at a moment that Soldi would be unable to pin down precisely, to plunge into the river of the outside world and let themselves be carried along, peacefully, by the current. Almost at the same time, Pigeon and Tomatis get to their feet, slowly, unaware as yet of the growing tumult round about them. Soldi seems to notice that their eyes meet, fleetingly, and almost immediately, for some reason that escapes him, they violent and more prolonged still than the first, echoes even more loudly in the patio, and it is the reverberations of it that seem to shake the tops of the trees, and not the wind that, in portions of the sky that the storm has not yet clouded over, sets the stars to twinkling. Pigeon's smile returns to his face, and he puts his hand in his pants pocket, preparing to pay.

"We're going to have to leave," he says, "because it's certain now that autumn is almost here."

**Other titles by Juan José Saer
and published by Serpent's Tail**

Nobody Nothing Never

'Now he dismounts, well in the background, underneath the eucalyptus trees, and laboriously frees the horse of its reins and saddle. The perforations of light that filter through the foliage leave spots on man and horse that move when they move. The whole ground is strewn with circles of light. I take the salami out of the refrigerator, the bread out of the sack. Tilty follows my movements as he talks.

"Night before last they killed another one in Santa Rosa," he says. "That makes nine."

"Ten," I say. "Last night they killed one here in Rincón . . ." '

During a stifling Argentinian summer, a horse-killer is on the loose. Cat Garay, heir to a once-prosperous, now dilapidated family, and his lover Elisa protect a horse from certain mutilation and death. An intense sexual affair and a desultory hunt for the killer are played out on the banks of the Paraná river in an atmosphere of political anxiety and disintegration.

The haunting prose of *Nobody Nothing Never* confirms Juan José Saer's reputation as the most innovative Latin American writer of his generation.

The Witness

A narrative: In sixteenth-century Spain, a cabin boy sets sail on a ship bound for the New World. An inland expedition ends in disaster when it is attacked by Indians.

A reflection on memory, on the role of objects in the construction of our world, on the relationship between existence and description, on foreignness, cultural identity and The Other.

A prose poem in the purest, most sensory language that remembers the forgotten contribution made by its native peoples to the creation of Latin America.

And the magnificent whole created by the author is far, far greater than the sum of its parts.

The verdict
on *The Witness*

'This haunting and beautifully written book travels an unexpected route. The author's preoccupations are reminiscent of his fellow Argentinians Borges and Cortázar but his vision is fresh and unique. I can't understand why, with the interest in things Latin American, we have had to wait so long for a book of his to appear in English.' *Independent on Sunday*

'A swashbuckling philosophical treatise that combines anthropology, semiotics and a dose of cannibal gore.' *Publishers Weekly (Best books of 1991)*

'There is no magical realism here, no baroque exoticism and not a particle of sentimentality that sometimes colours Latin American fiction, but instead an intensity of poetic description and the word "discovery".' *Times Educational Supplement*

'Shades of Melville and Conrad's *Heart of Darkness* influence an urgent narrative which unfolds through prose which has the terseness of reportage.' *Irish Times*

'Mr Saer's novel combines elements of the haunting metaphysical ambiguity of Jorge Luis Borges' poetry and Graham Greene's sensual description of the dark corners of the physical world and the human soul. The evocative imagery and ideas revealed in *The Witness* are not easily forgotten.' *Washington Times*

'Let me make myself clear: *The Witness* is a great book and the name of its author, Juan José Saer, must be added to the list of the best South American writers . . .' *Le Monde*

The Event

London, 1855, Bianco, the magician, is at the height of his powers. His telepathic gifts have made him famous throughout Europe – the Prussian secret service want to hire him to divine the secrets of their French counterparts. At a public meeting held to consecrate his fame, Bianco is undermined by a conspiracy of the Paris positivists. Exposed as a charlatan, he is forced to flee to the pampas of Argentina where he takes up with Gina whose voluptuousness matches her promiscuity. His career destroyed, his personal life riven with jealousy, Bianco descends into madness.

A fast page-turner, *The Event* is also an elegant reflection on the control of knowledge by the first world.